D0871935

ROUGE STREET

ROUGE STREET

Three Novellas

SHUANG XUETAO

Translated from the Chinese by Jeremy Tiang

Metropolitan Books

Henry Holt and Company   New York

Metropolitan Books
Henry Holt and Company
Publishers since 1866
120 Broadway
New York, New York 10271
www.henryholt.com

Metropolitan Books® and ⚏® are registered trademarks of
Macmillan Publishing Group, LLC.

Copyright © 2022 by Shanghai Translation Publishing House
Translation copyright © 2022 by Jeremy Tiang
All rights reserved.
Distributed in Canada by Raincoast Book Distribution Limited

"Moses on the Plain" (平原上的摩西) was originally published in the short
story collection with the same title by Thinkingdom/Baihua Literature and
Arts Publishing House, 2016.

"The Aeronaut" (飞行家) and "Bright Hall" (光明堂) were originally published in the
short story collection *The Aeronaut* by Imaginist/Guangxi Normal University Press, 2017.

Library of Congress Cataloging-in-Publication data is available.

ISBN: 9781250835871

Our books may be purchased in bulk for promotional, educational, or business use.
Please contact your local bookseller or the Macmillan Corporate and Premium
Sales Department at (800) 221-7945, extension 5442, or by email at
MacmillanSpecialMarkets@macmillan.com.

First U.S. Edition 2022

Designed by Kelly S. Too

Printed in the United States of America

1 3 5 7 9 10 8 6 4 2

This is a work of fiction. All of the characters, organizations, and events portrayed in this
novel either are products of the author's imagination or are used fictitiously.

CONTENTS

FOREWORD

Brutally funny, intricate, and alive, the three novellas that comprise *Rouge Street*—"The Aeronaut," "Bright Hall," and "Moses on the Plain"—teeter on a fulcrum between past and future. Behind is Mao's China, when the country's northeast stood at the heart of an industrial revolution; ahead, around the corner, is China's transformation into the economic superpower of the twenty-first century.

As one character in "Bright Hall" says: "Still the same people, though." The bullies, the bold, the dreamers, and the pragmatists all witness the collapse of state-owned factories, skyrocketing unemployment, and mass demolition of businesses and homes that mark the late 1990s. Rising and falling through a world of turbulent change, Shuang Xuetao's characters have surprising, often hidden, loyalties. The familiar world can dissolve instantaneously and whole spaces can disappear. What each chooses to remember constitutes their map of this world: the ground from which future decisions—split-second and momentous—will spring.

Yanfen Street, or Rouge Street, winds through Tiexi District, in the city of Shenyang, in the province of Liaoning. The district was settled by people thrown unceremoniously together—alleged class enemies and their equally despised children, former felons, hooligans, peasants, migrant workers, and the poor. Together, they formed a vast labor pool, disappearing into mines, smelters, and machine factories, tasked with building tractors or transformers, cleaning toilets, or making cigarettes. In "Bright Hall," Pastor Lin describes miners "recruited from among the downtrodden—rural migrants, unregistered households, demoted rightists, injured laborers—and corralled in Yanfen Township." All must settle, and attempt to thrive, in jobs they have not chosen.

In the twentieth century, Russia, Japan, Chinese warlords, and Chiang Kai-Shek fought bitterly for control of this area. Liaoning province, touching North Korea at one corner and Inner Mongolia at another, and sitting atop the Yellow Sea, is a location of strategic value. Every power that has occupied the region, with its coal mines and vast deposits of iron and magnesium, has capitalized on it as a source of raw materials and, later, as a center of heavy industry. Under Mao Zedong, the northeast rose to prominence as the "eldest son" of the nation. Smokestacks, chimneys, and factories ruled the landscape, accompanied by worker dormitories and shantytowns.

By the 1990s, Shenyang had a population of four million in an economy that was 85 percent state-run and heavily subsidized. In 1998, reform legislation came into effect, and companies were given three years to become profitable. A million people were soon laid off, losing not only their jobs but their health care and pensions. When factories closed, neighborhoods were demolished, people were relocated, and meager compensation was distributed, but only as a stopgap measure. Undreamed-of opportunities suddenly presented themselves for those with an entrepreneurial spirit and a willingness to play the game. But for millions of others, a very different state of existence arrived: that of being desperately poor while a select few, whose fates only yesterday had been tied to yours, grew wildly rich. A common world was fragmented into millions of individual pieces.

Earlier generations were told the story of a promised land, a communist future where workers would seize the means of production, triggering the end of capital and, ultimately, the end of class. The inheritance for this new man and woman, this new society, would be radical egalitarianism. In *Rouge Street*, residents tell gripping stories of the denounced, the resurrected, the ill-fated, and the stubborn, mingled with tales of prophets— Moses parts the waters, and Jonah is carried in the belly of a whale. The terrible and the miraculous can occur, but to what end? What if Moses parts the sea but leaves his people on the plain, far from the promised land, surrounded by walls of water?

Can a person, forced to fall, descend with dignity?

Shuang Xuetao (双雪涛), born in 1983, grew up on Yanfen Street in the city of Shenyang. The area is famously depicted in Wang Bing's documentary trilogy *West of the Tracks*, filmed with a rented handheld digital video camera from 1999 to 2001. Nine hours long, the trilogy shows the universe of life on Yanfen Street and in Tiexi District as "remnant factories" started to shut down and housing demolitions began. Wang Bing is one of the great filmmakers of our time. Film scholar Jie Li writes in *Jump Cut* that *West of the Tracks* "preserves the integrity of its disintegrating subject's time and space . . . and is edited into a narrative that maintains a humility of perspective rare in documentary treatments of the working class."

This is also a fitting description of Shuang Xuetao's writing. While employed at a bank in Shenyang, he wrote two well-received novels. He left Shenyang for Beijing's Renmin University, and began to focus on the short story form. His novella, "Moses on the Plain," the title story of his 2016 collection, was a sensation, catapulting him to literary stardom. A cascade of voices narrates "Moses on the Plain," which appears on the surface to be a detective tale. But here, as in Shuang Xuetao's other stories, surfaces quickly transform. Revelations do not result from new evidence but from the ripple effects of things long understood; events are driven by a resoluteness in each character—promises made, hidden bonds, a web of ethics that governs each life.

In *Rouge Street*, it's the nature of life for people to ask jolting questions, which I might paraphrase this way:

Do we pursue the past or the future, i.e., the head or the tail of the monster?

Who thinks without categories?

Can one rise in tumultuous times without stepping on the heads of others?

One should be bold, but how bold?

Knowledge is truth, labor creates freedom. Is that so?

Can you solve a puzzle and still not have the answer?

Who is our conscience?

Such questions, asked by individuals, are approached in ingenious ways in the structure of all three novellas. Reading "The Aeronaut" or "Bright Hall," we encounter a chessboard midgame. A long series of moves has already been made, and the outcome appears decided. There are no hidden spaces on a chessboard, no secret journeys, yet what seems inevitable can be swiftly overturned: individual pieces, each with their own isolating small or large problem to solve, have the potential to turn a game upside down. "Each of us has our own road to walk," says Master Li, one of the many souls who shape "Moses on the Plain." Every piece has limited power, sight, and possibility; but a fugitive can gain strength, or a man with a gun can be made powerless, depending on the configuration of the whole—a configuration that materializes not from thin air but from the communal architecture of the past.

Mathematics and probability are inherent to the structure of chess, yet just a few rules give rise to a dazzling tower of unknowns. *Rouge Street* is similar. Its stories feel like simple plains folded into interconnected infinity cubes. On the surface, Shuang's language is crisp and matter-of-fact. Here's Gao Xiaofeng, in "The Aeronaut," discussing his uncle:

According to my mother, after Uncle Mingqi's business failed, he was in the middle of gassing himself when he heard Grandpa grunting that he needed to pee. He went to help Grandpa, hugged him and wept for a while, and then decided to go on living.

But then time and space expand, even as the scene is confined to a small room, the crowded home of the Gao family: a woman makes dumplings for her husband; the husband nurses a drinking problem; a girl goes dancing with a boy wearing wide-bottomed pants; a man, who long ago promised to roast a rabbit for his boss, one night bathes his nine children before calmly committing suicide; a son improves the technology of a parachute; a boy is the unseen witness to a hilarious, wondrous drunken monologue. The narrative spins with panache and grace, regret and youthful dreams intersecting in the residents' tiny living quarters—the enclosure of a single story. The reader, buoyant, is bounced forward into the rest of their lives.

Like Gao Xiaofeng, the characters of *Rouge Street* tell it like it is, and this truth-telling is the surprising method by which his stories generate mystery. We can see the crime, the criminal, the victim, the setting, the motive, the facts, the interrogators—but this turns out to be a kind of tunnel vision. Shuang's approach is prismatic, aware of how the mind can fold decades of experience into an overpowering feeling, an instinct, a mission. Multiple characters remember the same long-ago event, but in recalling the past, each looks through a private keyhole shaped by their own experiences and values. The past, therefore, takes on a kind of elasticity, as idiosyncratic details begin to stand in for the whole. For the reader, the experience is thrilling: we are thrown through a series of paradigm shifts. We are granted more and more reality.

Late in *Rouge Street*, a character distills an idea that recurs in all three novellas: "My memory is great, it's just whether or not I choose to remember." This choice, in all its complexity, is the most powerful influence on how each individual faces the impossible. Loyalty—to a memory, a feeling, a friendship—is the shape-shifting mystery of *Rouge Street*, the spur for action. Out of loyalty, a police officer hesitates, an ethics teacher becomes a murderer, a man takes flight, a boy drowns, a doctor refuses to break under interrogation, and a good man exacts vengeance on the powerful. Loyalty to a memory is their defense against a rapidly changing world—it binds them to the streets that created them, and keeps that reality alive. To what will we be true? Who or what will we protect? We thereby stake a claim to our own lives.

The three novellas collected here assert that the fantastical is an intrinsic part of the real; that imagination and reason discover the world together. Shadow Lake, upon which "Bright Hall" turns, is aptly named: the lake of shadows, a tangible body accompanied by a play of light. Jeremy Tiang, who so brilliantly translates these works, asked Shuang about the origin of this lake—an expanse of absolutely clear water at the heart of Yanfen Street—which does not appear on any map. Shuang responded,

When I was little, there was a lake like that in Yanfen Street, though it wasn't really a lake, more a small pond. But it was a vivid jade green, the shape of a diamond, and left a deep impression on me. More recently, I asked my mom about it, and she didn't remember it at all— probably because it was so tiny. It was only because I was a child that I'd imagined it was enormous. So you could say that there was a real-life original for Shadow Lake, but it was very different from the Shadow Lake of the novella.

The novelist in me feels recognition: a pond in the shape of a diamond metamorphoses to occupy another realm. In "Bright Hall," the remembered pond becomes the portal of fiction, where space and time are reconfigured by narrative. Shuang's work is at ease with the fantastical, which is perhaps the disguise of the unsayable. What is the giant fish in "Bright Hall," the monster that swallows confessions, lives, and histories? How does it survive in a lake absent from all maps, a lake so crystalline it inspires wonder and fear? "Moses on the Plain" spirals toward an answer. We are carried forward and pushed under by connection and history, by solidarity and cruelty; we are entangled in collective movements so complex and far-reaching we have little chance to understand them—but each individual ultimately acts alone: do we paddle out into the lake to face our past? Do we heed the promises we made as children? Do we remember how we came to be?

Yanfen Street, as Shuang brings it to life, has a clarity that allows his characters to be seen in their full dimensions. The ground shifts beneath them; rising and falling force them into new perspectives. Only when the children in "Bright Hall" sink to the bottom of the lake do they see the foundation of their era—knowledge that, if they are fortunate, they will bring with them back to the surface.

—Madeleine Thien

TRANSLATOR'S NOTE

Born in the northeastern city of Shenyang, Shuang Xuetao spent much of his childhood in the neighborhood known as Yanfen Street, and may even have appeared in Wang Bing's famous documentary of the area. He recalls it as a run-down place of dirt roads and dingy houses. "Our neighbors were thieves, swindlers, con artists, drunkards, and gamblers," he said in a 2019 interview. "There were respectable people too, but you had to look quite hard to find them."

Yan (艳/yàn) means "bright," and fen (粉/fěn) means "powder." Yanfen, "bright powder," is not the usual way to say "rouge," but that is probably what is being referred to in the name Yanfen Street. The most common explanation comes from the early days of the Qing dynasty, when the surrounding land was used for the cultivation of plants that would be turned into makeup for the ladies of the imperial palace. The township became known as Yanfen (胭粉/yānfěn, "rouge powder"), before these syllables shifted into their contemporary meaning.

There are other legends about the name's origin. In one, a woman named Pear Blossom hung herself after being forced into marriage; red flowers bloomed on her grave. Another emphasizes a second century B.C. burial site in the Yan kingdom, suggesting that the current name is a corruption of the similar-sounding Yanfen (燕坟/Yānfén), meaning "Yan tomb."

Not all of Shuang's stories are set in Yanfen Street (the thoroughfare, less than two kilometers long, also lends its name to the surrounding neighborhood), yet his name is indelibly associated with this district, which exerts a presence over all his writing. In another interview, he said, "For me, Yanfen Street was like the American Wild West, a place inhabited by the downtrodden, lawless and free, and therefore full of life." He is also attracted to the contrast between the vibrancy of the name and the dull gray shantytown of his childhood, where the roads were puddled with mud, and the water and electricity might be cut off at any moment.

In 1995, the Shenyang singer Ai Jing released an album titled *Once upon a Time in Yanfen Street* whose title track features the refrain "Yanfen Street, so many stories happened here." The song also contains a verse recalling an incident she'd witnessed: a young man with long hair and flared trousers being denounced and paraded through the streets in disgrace because of his decadent fashion sense—an echo of the disapproval Li Mingqi faces in "The Aeronaut." In another verse, Ai Jing remembers lying on a stone bench, gazing at this dilapidated district, fantasizing about a future in which there are "more and more skyscrapers."

Indeed, Yanfen Street today is a bustling suburb of Shenyang, with orderly paved roads and many high-rise buildings. It may no longer be the disreputable, rough neighborhood of bygone days, but its wild spirit remains in Shuang Xuetao's writing, and so lives on.

—Jeremy Tiang

ROUGE STREET

THE AERONAUT

1

That morning in 1979 when Li Mingqi first showed up at his doorstep, Gao Likuan bristled, and not just at the boy's outlandish attire—although his bell-bottoms and flashy leather belt certainly didn't help. Gao had known Mingqi all his life, along with his two younger brothers and six little sisters; the family really was that large. The Lis lived in the row behind the Gao household, and beyond them was Red Flag Square, originally built by the Japanese, who paved it with marble from their quarry in Fuxin. When the work was done, the foreigners released a flock of pigeons into the square, which locals swiftly caught and took home for dinner. The next day, they released another flock of pigeons but stationed soldiers to guard them with rifles; that's how the Chinese learned that these birds were there to be fed, not eaten. The Japanese surrounded the square with banks and offices, abandoning the

structures when they departed. In 1967 a statue of Chairman
Mao was erected in the middle, and the pigeons all flew away,
never to return. Beneath the Chairman stood a squad of stone
soldiers led by a man with rolled-up sleeves who carried a great
crimson flag that billowed in the wind.

The Li house was another Japanese remnant, covering some
thirty-odd square meters, with a high ceiling and exquisitely
crafted windows. Though the printing company had provided
both the Gao and the Li homes, Li Mingqi's father had added
a loft to his, with five steps stuck into the wall leading up to it.
A family of eleven, women sleeping below and men above—
not a bad arrangement.

The main reason for Gao Likuan's annoyance, apart from
Li Mingqi's ridiculous clothes, was that Mingqi's father had
once been Gao's apprentice before going on to surpass him,
and it stung to have the man's son now courting his daughter.
Gao was a senior technician at the company, and there was
nothing he couldn't do—no printing problem ever daunted
him. He was also well respected: the foreman would offer him
a cigarette whenever they spoke, and even light it for him.
His status was due not only to his formidable skills but also
to his long-standing Party membership: born into hardship,
Gao Likuan had grown tired of people's sneers and joined
the Communists to print their leaflets. His leaflets were better than anyone else's, his colors more vivid, only growing
stronger with time. He had no schooling but learned to read
and write at the printing company, and after he'd picked up
enough words to turn a phrase, he would occasionally punch
up the managers' slogans to make them even more inspiring.
One of the bosses later sent him a letter saying he was proof
that great masters existed in every line of work, including

propaganda. He wasn't Master Gao yet—back then he was still Young Gao, and Young Gao spent two years printing leaflets, getting thrown in jail twice, first by the Nationalists and then by the Japanese. Both times he was beaten, so viciously the second that he was blinded in one eye, and subsequently he was known as One-Eyed Gao.

For some time after Liberation, One-Eyed Gao was happy: after all, it was a brand-new world, a brand-new era, even if he was still at the printing firm cranking out leaflets. It took a little longer for him to realize exactly what was so new about this world. The author of the complimentary letter was now the deputy mayor, and when he happened to think of Gao one day, he called the firm to ask if the propaganda genius was still around, or if he'd been martyred. The reply came: Yes, he's still around, and still printing leaflets, only he's lost an eye; he used to mix colors with two eyes, and now he does it with one, but the colors are just as bright. The deputy mayor sent someone to fetch him. They chatted for a while, and then the mayor announced that he was sending Gao off to cadre school. A few months of study, and Gao could be a deputy foreman. Gao Likuan said, I'm not presentable, I only have one eye, and anyway I'm no leader—I'm clumsy with words, I shake before crowds. I wasn't fit to be an officer during the Revolution, and now that we're in the New China, I'm very happy as I am, so why not continue as a worker? The deputy mayor replied, We owe you an eye, and that debt needs to be paid; besides, you have a bit of learning and your family background is impeccable—this is too good an opportunity to miss. Whether you want to or not, you're reporting to school tomorrow.

Gao Likuan felt distinctly uneasy after getting back from

City Hall, and asked his apprentice to come over for a drink. For his first visit to his mentor's home, Li Zhengdao brought half a chicken and a bottle of strong baigan liquor. They pulled the chicken apart while they drank.

—Zhengdao, this chicken isn't bad at all, where did you buy it?

—You can't buy this anywhere, sir. I roasted it myself.

—Why the hell are you still working in a factory? Open a restaurant—you'll make a fortune.

—It took me so long to roast this chicken, I'd just lose money. But of course I'm happy to do it for you, sir. Next time, I'll roast you a rabbit.

Gao Likuan was delighted—not only could his apprentice make a mean roast chicken, he knew what to say to make you feel good. Gao took a big swig of liquor and began to impart his wisdom about the printing business. Zhengdao listened with his head tilted to one side, now and then tearing off a particularly delectable morsel of chicken for his mentor. Gao, who was drinking quite quickly, finally remembered what he'd wanted to discuss.

—I was summoned to City Hall today. I don't feel good about it.

—How so, sir? When you got carried away in that big sedan chair, everyone just about lost their minds. Who knew you were an old revolutionary? You never said.

—Why the fuck would I say anything about it? If you have a big ass, you don't need to take off your pants to prove it.

—That's true.

—That courtyard in front of City Hall used to belong to the Japanese. That's where I lost my eye. There's still Japanese writing on the wall—they never painted over it. I don't want to go to cadre school, but I've got no choice; I can't offend the deputy mayor. I may only have one eye, but I can see clearly, and I know there's no point in me going. Why ask a fish to walk on land?

They drank late into the night, and though Zhengdao stayed over, Gao Likuan snored so thunderously, Zhengdao didn't get a wink of sleep. At dawn the next morning, he made Gao a large mug of tea and went off to work.

Gao turned out to be absolutely right—the wise have the gift of self-knowledge. The other people in the study session couldn't really read, and some were even less articulate than he was; they spoke their local dialect, which was intelligible only to themselves. One man was an opium addict and went into withdrawal halfway through a class, rolling around on the floor and twitching until they sent him home. Gao Likuan may have had a facial deformity, but his bearing was respectable— his shoulders were broad, his face was square—and though he couldn't speak as well as the professor, he could muster a couple of talking points when absolutely necessary. The mere fact that he separated his thoughts into points, rather than jumbling them all together like a bowl of congee, put him head and shoulders above the other students.

His problem was a weakness for liquor: he drank ten days out of the first fifteen, beat up a few classmates, and attacked an instructor who came to investigate. This wasn't just drunken violence; he also used the brawling skills he'd learned as a child from the old martial artists in North Market, which had gotten him through his two stints in prison. Beating up classmates was fine, but the instructor was older and had spent time in Yan'an, with bullet wounds that hadn't yet healed over, making him a far more credentialed revolutionary than Gao himself. Yet this instructor found himself dragged by the hair along a passageway, losing a chunk of his scalp in the process. Nursing his injuries, he stayed up all night writing a letter to the Party, pointing the finger at Gao, touching on every significant revolutionary event he could think of—the Taiping Heavenly Kingdom, the October Revolution, the Boxer Rebellion, the Yan'an Rectification Movement—to prove that thugs could be found even in a classless cohort and needed to be torn out by the roots. As a result, Gao Likuan was expelled and sent back to the printing company with his bedding roll, and this time there was no sedan chair; he had to travel by bus. Li Zhengdao took the bedding from him without asking any questions. To be honest, he knew from personal experience about his mentor's drinking habit. Once, Gao had gotten so worked up, he'd grabbed both Zhengdao and the chair he was sitting on and flung them out the window, into the street. And that was how Gao behaved when he had his freedom. It stood to reason that, cooped up in the cadre school, he would get bored and sneak out for a drink, leading, inevitably, to trouble.

Li Zhengdao was from Shandong. When his family couldn't feed themselves, and his parents grew too hungry to move, he had set off for the northeast with a bag of seeds to cultivate the land. After the river burst its banks in '40 and washed away his topsoil, he came to the city instead. First he worked in a secondhand bookshop, selling and appraising books by day, and taking the door off its hinges at night to serve as a makeshift bed. He learned to recognize a few words this way. Trying his hand at some more trades, he ended up at the printing company. Frankly, his proletarian credentials were also stronger than Gao Likuan's, except he'd never spent time in prison and had no complimentary letter from the deputy mayor. Even so, he could hold his liquor and never caused problems. He was alert and skillful with his hands, and he knew that the times had changed. As he saw it, the floodwaters had just receded, leaving a swath of bare soil. Here was his opportunity. That evening, Gao finally gave him an opening.

—Zhengdao, could you roast me a rabbit tomorrow?

—Okay, I'll bring it by your place tomorrow night.

—My hands do things they shouldn't. Now that I've hit someone, I deserve to be kicked out of the class, but the deputy mayor has stepped in to keep me there. He told me to think hard about what I've done and come back again next week. It's enough to torture a soul to death.

Zhengdao wiped a paper cutter and put it away in his toolbox. —Why don't I take your place?

Gao rose unsteadily to his feet. —You would do that?

—I can't bear to see you suffer like this.

—You'd have to stay there a whole month, stuck in a room all day hearing about Marx and Lenin. The gates are locked at night. Will you be able to stand it?

—I can try. If I fail, you can come and get me.

Gao spat on the floor. —All right then, I'll owe you one. I'll go to the municipal committee tomorrow and sort it out— where in Shandong are you from?

—Li Family Village in Shandong; my mother and father were both killed by the Japanese.

Zhengdao was being a little free with the truth there; his parents had actually starved to death, though if the Japanese hadn't invaded, if they hadn't conscripted men and confiscated rations, they probably would have had enough food, so it wasn't a complete lie, either.

Gao Likuan grabbed Li Zhengdao's hand and shook it heartily. Shaking hands was a new thing Gao had learned about in cadre school. My apprentice, he said, even if I get married and have children, you'll always be part of my family. After tomorrow, I'm not setting foot in City Hall again.

Zhengdao felt moved, and also a little guilty. He decided to make sure the roast rabbit the next day was extra delicious.

Li Zhengdao went to the class and really did disappear for an entire month. Gao Likuan resumed his bachelor lifestyle, working by day and drinking by night, donating nearly all his meager wages to the local bar. When he was done drinking, he'd go to the bathhouse for a soak, then lounge on the leather couch, taking a pumice stone to his feet, sipping strong tea, and chatting away late into the night. Ten days passed, and he'd all but forgotten there ever was such a person as Li Zhengdao. When Zhengdao came back after a month, his hairstyle had changed: it was longer now, neatly combed, and his little goatee had disappeared. He wore a blue polyester Mao suit. Right away, he made a beeline for the manager's office. Now, what is this, thought Gao Likuan, one lousy study class and you think you're brand-new? How dare you greet the manager before your mentor? When you're back in your worker's uniform, I'll deal with you!

He couldn't have dreamed that Li Zhengdao wouldn't put on a worker's uniform again for almost twenty years. First he was promoted to deputy director in Gao's workshop, implementing reforms in the production line and looking after some Russian clients, and then he became the chairman of the workers union for the entire factory, where he was charged with ideological reform. When they began rooting out rightist enemies of communism, Zhengdao was the first to write a denunciation, naming a few of the recalcitrant older printers. In short order, he was promoted to deputy factory manager, with every copy of *Chairman Mao's Selected Quotes* in the city printed under his supervision. He also traveled to nearby cities to give talks about how he had bettered himself.

Actually, Gao Likuan watched his ascent without ire—this was just his protégé's true substance revealing itself. Even if he hadn't gifted Li Zhengdao this opportunity, Li would have leaped into prominence sooner or later. After all, he never used notes when he spoke, and yet he was never less than eloquent, always ready with an apt quote from the Chairman. Moreover, Li Zhengdao continued politely addressing him as Mentor, and he never once lifted a finger against Gao through several campaigns. Gao called him Manager Li a few times, but he never allowed it, he would always say, Please, I'm just Zhengdao, without you there would be no me. That was good of him, Gao thought; he wasn't forgetting the wok after the food was eaten. Then two decades after his return from the cadre school, the Cultural Revolution arrived and knocked Li Zhengdao off his high horse. He wasn't thrown into the cowshed, nor was he made to clean toilets. They just ransacked his home several times, paraded him through the streets a little bit, made him assume the airplane position in a few struggle sessions, and shaved half of his head. He was removed from the coveted role of compiling Mao quotations and returned to the workshop, where he had to wear his uniform and resume the lowly work of operating the presses.

Over these twenty years, there were a few points where Gao thought Zhengdao had fallen short. First, he had children recklessly, nine of them in total. Once they popped out, he was so absorbed in his work that he didn't give a thought to raising them, so this gang of kids spent all day long running around the streets, stepping carelessly on the backs of their shoes, the big ones leading the little ones without discipline or order. Second, despite Zhengdao's promise that night, the roast rabbit never came. Gao suspected that rabbit would be more delicious than chicken, but even after waiting twenty years, he never got to taste it. Third, Zhengdao didn't come to talk it over before hanging himself. Dying is a major event, and you ought to discuss major events with other people, but Zhengdao didn't tell anyone. After getting beaten up yet again, he went home, gave all nine children a bath, then climbed up to the loft and put his head through a noose. All those years as a cadre, and such a selfish death. Gao had a lot to say about that.

And so when Li Mingqi showed up in '79, even if Gao's daughter hadn't introduced him, Gao Likuan would have known right away that this was Li Zhengdao's son. They looked exactly the same—tall and skinny, with a long, straight neck and deep-set eyes, like a foreign devil. After saying hello, Li Mingqi took out a handkerchief, wiped the seat of his chair, and sat down. He leaned his weight to one side, so that only a small patch of his white bell-bottoms touched the chair. Look at you, thought Gao Likuan, could you get any more uptight? Gao's daughter Yafeng was twenty-three and worked in the transformer factory. She wasn't exactly beautiful—her eyes bulged, her buckteeth pushed out her upper lip—but she was without question the most garrulous of the three Gao siblings. Even at her young age, once she got going, she would gab away for hours on end. That glib tongue persuaded her teacher to write a fake medical certificate, so she was never sent down to the countryside like all the other Educated Youths. After finishing junior high, she went straight into the transformer factory, earning over twenty yuan per month, more than anyone her age was getting. Yet on this day in 1979, Gao Yafeng sat by Li Mingqi's side not saying a word. She was scared of her father and, like a mynah bird confronted with a cat, knew that no amount of talk would help the situation. Her big sister Yachun was bustling around, stopping only to pour Li Mingqi a cup of tea, and Yafeng thought this was true sisterhood, to give her this show of respect in spite of how much they quarreled. She itched to list Li Mingqi's virtues, but when Gao Likuan's thick brows beetled together, she swallowed the words back down.

Gao Likuan drank a mouthful of tea, glanced at his wife, and finally spoke: Make a bowl of noodles, Boss. Zhao Suying, a diminutive, average-looking woman who also worked at the printing firm, was four years older than Gao Likuan. Her feet had once been bound, and she had been married before, but neither of these facts was fatal—Gao's missing eye made them an even match. Besides, her previous brief marriage was still childless when her husband died suddenly. After marrying into the Gao family, she had a baby every three years, two girls and then a boy, which pleased Gao. The only problem was Suying's slow nature—she could spend half an hour walking between two telegraph poles. A crisis could be raging, and she'd still be asleep on the heated platform of the kang bedstove. Gao roughed her up when he'd had too much to drink, but that didn't make her move any faster. When he was done but still furious, she'd sweep up the broken bowls and chopsticks, then sit down and listen to opera on the radio: *Mu Guiying Takes Command*. Gao Likuan found himself thinking about China's former capitalists, who'd assumed they'd come out on top in the New China, only to get held up by slow workers like her. So he gave her a nickname: Boss. Now the Boss stood up from her stool and went to the kitchen for a noodle board, which she put on the side of the kang, then back again for an aluminum basin covered with muslin that reeked of alkaline. We'll have dumplings today, said Suying. That startled Gao. Suying held the purse strings, because the boss controls the money; that's the natural order of things. He wasn't even sure where she kept the savings book. All he knew was that she had some petty cash wrapped in her handkerchief, and when he wanted to get some liquor, she'd untie the knot and hand him a banknote. If they were having dumplings, she must have bought the ingredients specially. He felt conflicted. On one hand, he didn't think they ought to treat Li Mingqi like an honored guest. On the other hand, dumplings paired excellently with liquor. As he mulled this over, he hauled out the small square table from under the kang and set it up in the middle of the platform.

2

I'd only just fallen asleep when Eldest Aunt called. Finding myself still wide awake at three in the morning, I'd gone downstairs for a case of beer and worked my way through three bottles before finally feeling drowsy. I flung myself into bed right away but didn't manage to doze off. The beer swelled my stomach, and I got up again at five for an epic piss. Winters in Beijing were different from back home— the days were thick with fog, and although the temperatures weren't as low, the damp chilled you to the bone. At night, frosty air seeped through the window cracks. The beer was making mischief, and I started to shiver, burrowing deeper into the blankets. The next day was Saturday, and I was supposed to play indoor soccer with my supervisor. I'd been quite the soccer star in college, a right winger with a killer feint. Since then, I'd gained a paunch, and simply putting on workout clothes made me break out in a sweat. Thankfully, the point was the beer we would have afterward—or not the beer so much as listening to my supervisor rant about how he, too, had been a soccer star in college, when he could pass a ball more than seventy meters. To endure it, I'd hoped to stay in bed at least till dawn.

Around seven-thirty, I fell into a deep sleep. I forgot I was in a rented room near the Fourth Ring Road. My jaws clenched as I was transported back to that hard single bed at home; then the bed vanished and I was in a university entrance-exam hall, but somehow I couldn't answer the politics questions, and when I craned my neck to see what other people were doing, they were all very far away, shielding their papers with their hands. I felt frantic beyond words. That's when the phone rang—I sat bolt upright.

—Ah? Is that Xiaofeng?

Right away I knew it was my eldest aunt. We hadn't spoken in two years, but her Jinzhou accent was so distinctive, always flicking up at the end of a phrase, as if she were singing. Also, she didn't say hello—she said ah, as if it was a big surprise when someone answered her call.

—Aunt Yachun.

—Wretched child, not calling me at New Year's. Your grandma says she misses you every day.

—I haven't slept, Aunt, can I call you back later?

—Don't worry, I didn't call to ask for my money back. This is about something else.

I'd been afraid she would bring this up. Eldest Aunt had paid my college fees—I'd graduated five years before and had not yet repaid her. Actually, it was thirty thousand yuan, which I could have returned by now, but when she'd given me the money she'd said it was a gift, not a loan. I'd thought that what I owed her was my gratitude. As the best off among Pa's siblings, Eldest Aunt was happy to be the head of the family. She got in touch with me from time to time, urging me to visit my grandma. Jinzhou isn't too far from Beijing, but there's absolutely nothing to do there, and my grandma became so addled after turning eighty, seeing her was the same as not seeing her. So I never went. Once Eldest Aunt said to me on the phone, I'm not asking you to pay me back, I just want you to see your grandma, you're her only grandson, she's your only grandma, and when she's dead—someone her age could die from as little as a fart, you know—you'll only be able to see photos of her. I agreed to visit her right away, but then got annoyed as soon as we hung up, and I never did go. That she refused repayment was really a masterstroke—it made me act on her terms.

—Send me your account details, Aunt, and I'll make a bank transfer. It's been a few years, so to take inflation into account, I'll send you forty thousand.

—You don't listen to half of what I say, child. I'm not talking about money. This is important.

—What is?

—Your Uncle Mingqi has gone missing. Your cousin Li Gang, too.

My mouth went dry, but there wasn't any water around, so I took a swig of last night's beer.

—Missing? What do you mean?

—I mean they're nowhere to be found. They both went out early on Friday morning for tofu pudding, and then they disappeared.

—Did you make a police report?

—Don't you know what kind of person your cousin is? He only just got out of prison last year. And listen, before Li Mingqi ran off, he borrowed money from his neighbors, and now they're knocking on his door every day. So let's put our heads together and sort this out as a family. We'll only involve the law if necessary.

—All right, then. You take the train to Shenyang, and I'll provide backup from here in Beijing.

—Listen, you brat, I've had a slipped disk for the last five years, all from taking care of your dying father, and now I'm having to look after your grandma. Get yourself to Shenyang or I'm sending her back.

This was a reference to back when Pa had cancer. Ma was at her wit's end, and I'd only just got into college, so Eldest Aunt came over from Jinzhou to help out. One night, she was lifting Pa to examine him when she threw her back out, and she never fully recovered. After Pa's death, she looked at the state of our household and brought my grandma away to live with her, taking a huge load off our shoulders.

—I'm not trying to avoid my responsibilities, Aunt, but I studied law, and now I'm working in legal services at a bank, nothing to do with criminal investigation. This isn't my area of expertise. Anyway, Grandma is used to living with you, and you yourself said how frail she's getting; she probably couldn't stand to be moved. Let's not make any decisions while we're upset.

—Oh, so now you're all grown up, you think you can tell your aunt how to act? Make no mistake, you're coming back right away to find your uncle and cousin. If not, I'm buying your grandma a train ticket, and she can stage a one-woman protest at your workplace. She may be confused, but her legs are sturdier than mine.

And with that, she hung up. I called my supervisor and told him I wouldn't be at that afternoon's soccer game, then gritted my teeth and asked for a week off. I'd actually promised this vacation time to my mother—we were supposed to go to Hong Kong. She spent all day watching TVB dramas and wanted a trip to Hong Kong to try the packed lunches there. I was looking forward to it too, to be honest. I wanted to visit Disneyland and ride those machines that toss you through the air. Some people are scared of heights, but my family has never been. In fact, a weird thing about us: we actually enjoy being high up. When Pa was still around, every time he got upset with Ma, he'd go sit on the roof. Ma would say, What, are you a monkey in disguise? He wouldn't respond, would just sit there till it was dark, and when he came down, his anger would be gone. My supervisor was unhappy that I was asking for vacation—I still had six or seven contracts on my desk that I hadn't finished going through. But in three years, I hadn't asked for a single day off. Meanwhile, my supervisor flew his wife and kids to what seemed like half the holiday destinations in the world, sometimes calling from abroad to order me to work late. So he didn't resist, just told me to not get too distracted.

It was seven in the evening by the time I arrived in Shenyang. There was no one at home, but the rice cooker was warm, and the dishes drying by the sink still had water droplets on them.

December in Shenyang is serious winter. My parents' home was in an old housing development where the heat was controlled centrally, so no one paid for it. The management company was afraid that if they didn't give us any heat at all, people might freeze to death and make headlines, so they supplied just enough that you could warm your hands on the radiators. Ma's red wool slippers were on the floor, so battered they looked like a couple of roast yams. Those were the ones I bought her at Muji, on my first New Year visit after I started working. Ma said I shouldn't have given her footwear, that it was like hinting that she should hit the road and remarry. I said I didn't mean that at all; they were a pragmatic choice. Ma's feet were terribly dry, and her heels cracked in the winter, trapping fibers from her socks, and this looked highly uncomfortable. I'd been too busy for the past couple of years to pay much attention to her feet, so I didn't know if they'd improved since I'd given her the slippers.

I went into my room: a single bed, a bookcase, a swivel chair, an old desk lamp. The wardrobe behind the chair used to be taller than me; now it came up to my chin. On top of it was my savings bank, a grinning piggy. I sat down for a moment. It had been more than six months since my last visit. I pulled open a desk drawer: fountain pen, ink, a remaindered cassette tape I bought in junior high—some white guy playing a saxophone. My visits were always so rushed, I hadn't opened this drawer in quite a while. Farther in were homework books from when I was a kid, and every greeting card I'd received from elementary school to senior high. I flipped through them slowly. Near the back, just as I remembered, I'd hidden a note: *Ling, last-minute trip today. Make dinner for Xiaofeng. Steamed buns in the fridge. Xuguang.* Before Pa got sick, near the end of his working life, he was often sent out to various villages to repair tractors. He'd left this note on one of those occasions. Pa did the cooking in our household, which was maybe a bit unusual.

The window faced east. Across the way was a large hotel that blocked out most of our daylight. Only in the evening were the rays of the setting sun reflected at just the right angle to reach a little into our apartment. That night, about a third of the windows were lit up, mostly with their curtains drawn closed. Through one set of curtains that was open, I saw a chambermaid gripping a blanket with both hands, flicking it vigorously so it spread and settled over a pure white double bed.

The door slammed shut. I closed the drawer and came back out. Ma was taking off her shoes. Another clump of her hair had turned gray, and the bags under her eyes were heavier than I remembered. Her figure hadn't changed, though—she was still a little plump, resembling a brown bear in her faded red down jacket. She looked up at me.

—Why are you back?

—Ma, did you know that my uncle and cousin have gone missing?

—Yes, your aunt called me a couple of days ago. Have you had dinner?

—I ate at the train station. How do two grown men just go missing like that?

—Tell me, how many words have you spoken to your uncle and cousin in the last decade?

I thought for a moment. —We talked after Grandpa died, and then again when Pa died. I can't really think of any other times.

—Right. And when your father was ill, how many times did they visit?

—I don't remember.

—Once. He was in the hospital for a month, couldn't even speak, and they came once. Stayed for twenty minutes, brought him a bag of apples and a bunch of bananas, and tossed us two hundred yuan. One time.

—I forgot.

Ma jabbed a finger at her skull. —I've never had a good memory. Even as a kid, I was always losing things. But I'll never forget something like that. Every single incident, laid out under a light.

—Under a light?

—I can see them so clearly, as if they're under a light.

— I'm going to see Aunt Yafeng tomorrow. Do you want to come?

She glared at me. —Is that why you're back?

—Yes, Aunt Yachun phoned me this morning.

—You asked for time off?

—Annual leave.

—So we can't go to Hong Kong?

Feeling a little guilty, I walked over and patted her on the arm. —Next year, Ma.

—Fine. If your father wasn't dead, I wouldn't be pinning my hopes on you.

With that, she went into her room and locked the door.

Ma used to be a very warmhearted person. According to my father, she had been a ray of sunshine in her youth. A bit willful, but adorable. She had a long black plait, cheated at poker, and smiled at everyone she met. After the factory went bankrupt and the two of them had to fend for themselves, her spirits grew a little heavier. When their home was demolished in the government's urban clearances, and they had to move to a shantytown on the outskirts of the city, her spirits grew heavier still. They were given a new apartment in compensation, but it never got any sunlight, no one ever cleaned the shared corridors, and the young renters upstairs were professional thugs. Then my father died, a blow that completed Ma's descent into dour middle age. She hadn't entirely given up on life, though. Wanting to go to Hong Kong was a sign of this—a shame I had to let her down. The more I thought about it, the more I hated this stinking plan Eldest Aunt had mixed me up in.

Ma's door was still shut the next morning. I listened outside for a while. She must have been awake, but I didn't hear the TV. I went looking for something to eat and found some rice already cooked, along with a dish of tomato-egg stir-fry and a small bowl of steamed egg, keeping warm in the rice cooker. A brown notebook sat on the dining table. I opened it and saw a bunch of phone numbers and addresses in my father's handwriting. Second Aunt's details looked at least a decade old—I hoped they were still accurate. *From the east side of TieDep, turn right at the first hutong, right again when you see a shop selling cloth shoes, go up to the third floor of Block 2, and it's the black Panpan security door.*

TieDep meant Tiexi Department Store, which was in the

center of Tiexi District. I'd been there as a child. It got really
crowded on Sundays. Across from the shopping center was a
Xinhua Bookstore with two racks of books to browse—you had
to ask a clerk if you wanted to see the rest behind the counter.
A few pages of my father's booklet were filled with lists of numbers: *ball bearings—6, screws—8 boxes, hinges—7 boxes, gas—3
buckets*. And underneath: *to get*. Probably left over from when
he was a laborer. I knocked on the bedroom door and said,
Ma, I'm taking the notebook. No response. I heard the curtains rustling but couldn't tell if she was opening or closing
them. I put on my down jacket and left.

Almost nothing had changed. The crossroads were still
there, though the Xinhua Bookstore had been replaced by a
Pizza Hut. Tiexi Department Store was gone too, and a small
supermarket stood in its place. I stopped by for a couple of
cartons of milk. The cloth-shoe shop was still there, and it now
made burial clothes, too. A few old men sat in the courtyard
chatting, all bundled up in hats and gloves. Block 2. Third
floor. Sure enough, there was a black Panpan door, with little
ads stuck all over it, like a piece of pop art. Next to the door
was a wooden Sanyuan milk crate, on which was written: *Gao
Yafeng*. I rapped on the door. No answer. I tried again. A voice:
Who's there?

— Second Aunt?

—Who's there?

—Xiaofeng. Gao Xiaofeng. Your nephew.

—My nephew?

Slippers shuffled toward the door. The voice again: Could
you pull the ad off the peephole? I obeyed, and the voice said,
You really are my nephew. The door opened.

Second Aunt looked small and wizened, and her thinning

hair had been combed to one side, making it look even sparser. Her cheeks were recessed, and age spots covered her face. She'd lost quite a few teeth, and when she smiled, her gums glistened. The layout of the apartment was as I remembered: living room in the middle, with bedrooms to the north and south. Her feet dragged as she led me into the southern one. The other belonged to my cousin—I'd played there as a child, and slept in his bed. But that door was closed at the moment. There were two steamed buns on the bed in the southern room, one half-eaten, revealing its filling of pickled vegetables and egg, the other hard as a clump of concrete. On the TV, a woman was singing. I knew that my aunt had rheumatism and found it hard to go out, and now that I thought about it, I'd learned that a very long time ago, though it felt like just yesterday. With crooked fingers like chicken feet, she set down a glass of water in front of me, and I handed her the milk in exchange.

—Just come if you're coming, no need to bring anything. How's your mother?

—Not too bad, Aunt Yafeng.

—Do you prefer singing or movies? We could switch to the movie channel.

—Aunt Yafeng, I got a phone call from Aunt Yachun.

—Last time I saw you would have been your father's funeral. Five years ago?

—Five years ago.

—It was winter then too, wasn't it? I cried so hard. I stayed home all those years, then the moment I leave the house, I let myself down like that. Shame on me.

—What are you talking about, Aunt? It would be weird if you hadn't cried.

Second Aunt's room was tiny and immaculate. The carpet

was no longer red, but it didn't have a speck of dust on it. She wore a black padded jacket, slightly too large for her, the cuffs spotless. Her red socks looked brand-new, too. She jabbed a finger toward the window.

—Xiaofeng, you see that chimney?

I craned my neck to look. A chimney was indeed there, dull red and about a hundred meters away, not emitting any smoke, metal rungs fitted along one side.

—That's what blocked your uncle.

—I'm not sure I understand, Aunt.

—That cursed chimney stood in the way and blocked all the good energy. That's why he never got well.

I said nothing.

—Now you've made something of yourself, you're a respectable man in Beijing. Go talk to someone, get that chimney torn down.

—Aunt, I may be in Beijing, but I'm just a bank worker; I'm not in charge of chimneys. Look, there's no smoke coming from it, and the ladder's all rusted. Leave it alone, and someone will tear it down soon enough.

—That's what I thought, but it's been fifteen years, and it's still there blocking me. I phoned your mother a couple of days ago, and she said you're a big shot, you have dinner with Wang Qishan. You mean to tell me you can't get rid of one wretched chimney?

—Ma was exaggerating—I've only seen Vice President Wang on TV. And if I were that high up, having dinner with him would probably be bad news, don't you think?

Second Aunt was silent for a moment. —I shouldn't have danced.

—What?

—Dancing ruined my life.

—I thought it was the chimney?

She picked up the steamed buns and examined them, then set them down again.

—The chimney is one thing, dancing is something else. I went dancing when I was young, and that's how I met your uncle—the first ruination. This was after work, when I would dance all night and go to work the next day still covered in sweat. The wind hit me and sent a chill into my joints, and that's how I got rheumatism. Second ruination. I taught your uncle to dance, and he kept going after I had to stop, dancing all the way out of my life. Third ruination. Are you hungry, Xiaofeng? Help yourself.

I was, so I went into the living room and opened the fridge. Every inch of it was crammed full of steamed buns. I closed the door again and turned back to Aunt Yafeng. Her eyes were fixed on the woman singing on the TV, her toes lightly tapping to the beat.

3

The Boss wielded the cleaver and began chopping the filling for the dumplings. Gao Yachun knew her mother was a woman of few words—you could hold a knife to her throat, and she'd still think for a good while before asking for mercy. Not wanting to offend Li Mingqi, Yachun searched for a topic of conversation. As a nurse trainee, she was the highest-educated person in the family, which gave her the authority to speak out. She knew her sister Yafeng was a shallow person—when they'd tried to set her up before, the matchmaker would proclaim the guy's education and family wealth, but all Yafeng wanted was his photo. This concerned Yachun, who insisted on chaperoning the first few dates. If the guy was just a pretty face—a lousy pillow in a nicely embroidered case—she'd halt proceedings immediately. Yachun herself was getting married soon, to the medical student next door who was being deployed to Jinzhou as a doctor. He was plain and dutiful, and the whole family approved of him. They would go through the ceremony in Jinzhou that fall. All that summer, Yachun's heart was a knot of worries. First of all, she was moving far away—Jinzhou was in the same province but a six-hour train ride away, so she wouldn't be able to visit easily. She fretted about her family. Second, she didn't know a soul in Jinzhou and would have to start from scratch. She'd heard about Bijia Mountain, an island near Jinzhou that was connected to the mainland by a path at low tide, so you could simply walk there—but if you didn't make it back before the tide turned, the path would disappear under the waves, and you'd be trapped. When she thought about going all the way to Jinzhou to put down roots, she felt uneasy. Third, she planned to knit each of her family members a sweater before she went, but time was growing short, and she wasn't finished. She reached into her bag for the tieguanyin tea leaves she'd asked a friend to get her from Tiexi Department Store, and went into the outer room to brew them. She poured Gao Likuan and Li Mingqi a cup each. Mingqi leaned forward, raising his behind slightly off the chair, and said, Sis, please don't bother. From this close up, his appearance was perfectly acceptable: thick brows, large eyes, an aquiline nose, lashes at least an inch long that fluttered like a couple of butterflies. Yachun said:

—Mingqi, I hear you're working at the arsenal?

—That's right.

—That's a good job. I suppose it's all top secret?

—Not really. I can't tell you exactly what I do, but basically we make parachutes.

—Parachutes?

—There are quite a few workshops, all related to airplanes. Mine does parachutes.

All of a sudden, she found him dashing. Yachun said:

—I heard you were responsible for some progress last year?

—It was nothing much. I invented something, a small component that improved the parachute.

Now he was even more impressive, a veritable Edison. Yafeng chose this moment to butt in. And that's not the half of it, she said. Gao Likuan looked sidelong in her direction. Meanwhile, her brother, Gao Xuguang, had been reading—he was quite the bookworm. He'd read big-character protest posters during the Cultural Revolution, and the dictionary when he was sent down to the countryside. Back in the city, he was deployed to the tractor factory, but he went to the library as soon as he got off work. Like his mother, he seldom spoke, not even about the books he read; he just pondered those alone. Gao loved his young son and often said two things. The first was: Boss, if you hadn't given birth to Xuguang, you'd have suffered much more. The second: Boss, our printing company relies on people like Xuguang, people who like words, to stay in business. At this moment, Xuguang raised his head too, as he waited to hear what Mingqi would say next. Mingqi drank a mouthful of tea before speaking.

—Well, it *was* a small component, but its function was crucial. Essentially, it makes the parachute open faster than before, and reduces the overall weight. It's a bit heavier than what the Americans have, but it's very close. No one dared to try it out, so I did.

Xuguang closed his book. —How so?

—I jumped out of a plane at five thousand meters. There was a bit of a problem—a switch got stuck and I had to fiddle with it—so my chute opened three seconds later than planned. I missed the target and landed in a tree. The second time went better, so I was credited with the achievement.

Gao Likuan thought, This kid is just like his father—eager to climb, doomed to fall. Listening to this story, Yachun shook nervously. As a nurse, she knew that a fall of five thousand meters would smash you to a pulp. Even landing in a tree could mean broken bones. She said:

—How about you just stick to inventing things in the future, and skip the experiments? You were lucky this time around, but you might not be next time—you never know.

Yafeng laughed. —It's not that he was lucky; his bones are light. When I go dancing with him, he takes the woman's part and I lead. I only have to tug a little, and he spins.

Yachun glared at her, and Yafeng shut her mouth. Mingqi said:

—It's true, I'm lighter than most people, not in terms of weight, but somehow I become buoyant. When I was a kid, my father used to take me kite flying. One time, he fashioned a huge centipede. The wind was strong, and my kite lifted me into the air—I flew a hundred meters with my feet off the ground, and only stopped when I hit a mailbox. Pa never took me kite flying again.

Gao Likuan knew about this kind of kite. It used a special type of paper, which he'd manufactured. This mention of Li Zhengdao made his heart clench. His apprentice had been so quick-witted and dexterous—such a pity he'd died, leaving behind a huge litter of children. Mingqi, the eldest, was helping his mother bring up the younger eight. Despite the turbulent times, not a single one of them had died, and he himself was making parachutes at the arsenal—what an achievement! Gao thought about how he'd spent so many years being angry with Li Zhengdao, and how he hadn't lifted a finger to help the family, hadn't so much as lent them a scoop of soybean oil. He saw how a big, tall man like himself could have a heart smaller than the eye of a needle, and he sighed, blinking with his single eye.

At her father's sigh, Yafeng got flustered, thinking she must have annoyed him with her talk of dancing. She nudged Mingqi with her eyes toward the army bag at the head of the kang. From it he took out two bottles of Western Phoenix liquor. When Gao Likuan saw the offering, he swung his legs onto the kang, pointed at Mingqi, and said, Come sit here. Yachun had no idea her father wore a halo of guilt. She believed that although he was the head of the household, his inner workings were simple, and this gift would be all it would take to win him over—as Chairman Mao said, a candy-coated bullet to pierce his heart. She thought again that she would soon be married and living far away, and grew even more anxious for her family. Mingqi stood and tried to climb onto the kang, but his trousers were too tight to let him sit cross-legged. He said:

—I'll join you by the side of the kang, Uncle. My father left these two bottles of liquor. He wanted to save them, so he buried them in the yard, and no one found them when they were ransacking our house. Let's drink as much as we can today, and you can keep what's left.

—How much can you drink?

—It depends. If I've had enough sleep, at least half a bottle.

—Not bad, then we won't have any left. Boss, forget the dumplings and fry us some peanuts. We'll take a little break.

Zhao Suying put down her knife, wiped her hands on her apron, and went to light the stove in the outer room. Xuguang started to leave. Mingqi said:

—Aren't you having a drink?

Xuguang looked back. —I hate this sort of thing.

With that, he took his book and left the room. It was noon, and the summer sun was directly overhead. Xuguang climbed the ladder onto the roof, reclined on the slope, and reopened his book. In his early teens, Xuguang had made two resolutions: first, he would never touch a single drop of alcohol, and second, he would never raise a hand against his wife, no matter how much she aggravated him. If he really couldn't stand it, he would leave. At that young age, he'd staged a revolution deep in his soul and swept everything to do with Gao Likuan out the door.

The peanuts were served, the glasses laid out. Gao Likuan said, Let's have one more. And so another appeared. Gao filled all three and spoke again.

—Zhengdao, life is strange. Who'd have thought I'd spend all those years craving your roast rabbit, only to sit with your son, drinking the liquor you left? I guess that's fate. You left early, and I'll go too, sooner or later. You're the bigger man because you went first, so here's a toast.

Having nothing better to do, Yafeng sat on the bench hugging her knees, watching the men drink. That afternoon, she held back a whole bellyful of words, which felt even worse than holding back piss—you can always pee your pants, but if it becomes too hard to hold back your words, you can't

just stand up and shout them out. Gao Likuan never let the
women join him when he was drinking. They either had to
wait till he was done and eat his leftovers or grab some food to
eat on their own. Zhao Suying usually ate standing up at the
stove. She was small and skinny, and didn't have much of an
appetite—a couple of mouthfuls satisfied her. Right now, she
was boiling some dumplings. Xuguang was allowed to join his
father, but he always refused. As a result, if Gao Likuan was
home for dinner, he'd eat alone, then drink alone for several
hours, until he keeled over on the kang. Seeing her father and
Mingqi drinking, Yafeng felt a flaming anxiety. Now they'd
keep going till midnight, and she'd have to hold these words
in her belly till then. Her legs jiggled. Meanwhile, Yachun
was unraveling one of Xuguang's old, holey sweaters to knit
a new one. Yafeng stuck out her hands for her sister to wind
the wool around. After thinking for quite a while, she finally
found something to say.

—Pa's going to get completely smashed today.

—Let him, as long as he's happy.

Yafeng nodded. Her big sister knew how to swallow her
anger.

Neither man said anything when the dumplings were
served. They'd already had several glasses of liquor each, and
Mingqi's expression was unchanged as he brought the peanuts
to his mouth. This cheered Gao—no one in his family would
drink with him, and this kid knew how to handle himself: he
always made sure his glass was a little lower than Gao's when
they toasted, and here he was serving him the hotter dumplings and taking the cold ones for himself. Gao said, Boss,
these dumplings aren't bad. Zhao Suying didn't hear him.

She'd gone up the ladder with a mug of water for Xuguang, and was waiting there for him to finish it. Her son said:

—Ma, is Li Mingqi still drinking?

—He can hold his liquor. Move over a bit, it's scorching.

—I'd like some dumplings too, Ma.

—I made some with shrimp for you. I'll bring them up in a minute.

—Three drops of soy sauce, four drops of vinegar.

Zhao Suying nodded and climbed back down the ladder.

Gao Likuan guzzled another couple of glasses, and the room grew fuzzy. This was his optimal state of being, when everyone looked pleasing to his lone eye. He said:

—Young Li, your father called me Mentor, but what do you call me?

—I call you Uncle.

Gao waved this away. —You ought to call me Mentor, too.

Eavesdropping from her perch, Yafeng thought this hierarchical thinking sounded absurd. Mingqi said:

—My father learned printing from you, but I'm at the arsenal, so your skills won't do me any good.

Gao waved that away, too. —I'll teach you something else today, and then I *will* be your mentor.

He reached out and picked up the cleaver from where Zhao Suying had left it on the edge of the kang. The Gaos had a picture of Chairman Mao stuck to the back of their front door, red-cheeked and grinning, face like an overripe apple. Gao said, Look at his left eye. The cleaver hurtled through the air and lodged itself in that very mark. Mingqi noticed that the Chairman's face was covered in knife wounds—this must be a frequent performance. He said:

—I'll never be able to do that, I don't have the strength.

—What do you mean? Give me your hand.

Mingqi put his palm out, soft and white like a girl's. Gao took it and yanked him to the side. Unexpectedly, Mingqi arced through the air, crash-landing under the window like a sack of flour.

Yafeng dropped the wool and jumped to her feet. —Pa, what the hell are you doing?

Mingqi sat up and crawled back to his spot. —I'm fine, I'm fine. Just a bit shaken, not hurt.

Gao swung his hand through the air. —Why are you so light?

—I told you, I have light bones.

Gao kneaded Mingqi's shoulder. —I feel bones there.

—Yes, I have bones, but they're hollow. Maybe it's because I was born in a loft.

Yachun, with her medical knowledge, knew perfectly well that hollow bones had nothing to do with where you were born, but she didn't correct him. Gao said:

—No wonder falling from five thousand meters didn't kill you; you're a flea on a drum. Let me teach you qinggong— weightless martial arts.

—Sure, that I could use.

Seeing that Mingqi was fine, Yafeng sat back down. The two men filled their glasses and made another toast.

Mingqi could manage only one bottle of liquor. Up to that point, he was humble and cautious, and could refrain from bragging or losing his temper. If he drank more than one bottle, he would begin to reveal his true self, speaking without inhibition. When he hit a bottle and a half, he simply collapsed, becoming insensible to the world. Yafeng didn't know this about him, because they had met at a dance hall, and though they'd have a drink or two while they were dating, Mingqi never let himself go. Yafeng, too, stuck to beer, just enough to cut loose; if she'd had too much and Gao had smelled it on her when she got home, he'd lash out at her. So when Mingqi's expression began to shift after the first bottle of liquor, she didn't notice. The sun had set by now. Xuguang had eaten his dumplings on the roof and was asleep with his book over his face. Gao Likuan and Li Mingqi had exchanged a lot of words this afternoon, covering everything from Chiang Kai-shek to Du Yuesheng, from the Gang of Four to Ye Jianying, from the wonders of Japanese plumbing to Tanaka Kakuei, the prime minister when Japan and China were establishing diplomatic relations. Stubborn as Gao had been all his life, Mingqi defeated him in conversation that afternoon. For everything Gao knew in broad outlines, Mingqi had the fine detail; Gao had read the newspaper headlines, but Mingqi knew the inside pages; Gao's knowledge covered this patch of land, but Mingqi's left the hutong, took a turn, and reached as far as Shanhaiguan. Gao had never admired anyone, but that afternoon he admired Li Mingqi. Such determination, in one so young. No wonder he wore bell-bottoms—only wide-legged pants could fit so much knowledge.

Finally, they got to talking about Li Zhengdao. Mingqi said:

—Before my father killed himself, he gave all nine of us kids a bath. I went last, and took the longest, because he had things he wanted to say to me.

—Like what?

—He told me that I wasn't doing badly as the oldest son, that I knew how to take care of my brothers and sisters, but there was one area where I could improve, and that was making more of myself, to set a good example. We only get one life; some die in bed, others die on horseback, and if you have the chance to die on horseback, then do so. Be a Napoleon in this world. Even if you're a watermelon seller, then be the Napoleon of watermelon selling.

Gao felt even more defeated—he would never be a Napoleon. Still, having a Napoleon in his family might be enough to make people look at him differently.

—If you were to marry Yafeng, where would you live?

This question turned Li Mingqi from Napoleon back into Li Mingqi. He hung his head.

—I have nowhere to live, Uncle. My brother moved out after he got married, but there's still nine of us at home.

—You can live here. Yachun's leaving for Jinzhou in a couple of days. There's room.

Yafeng was stunned. Today was only supposed to be a normal visit. Li Mingqi boasted his looks and his job, but his merits stopped there. If they hadn't already slept together, lowering her value, she wouldn't even have brought him home to stroke the tiger's rump. This was like trying clothes on for size only to find she'd somehow already bought the outfit, and the salespeople were throwing a lambswool coat into the bargain. She hastily tried to work out if they were even compatible. Mingqi was clever but a bit too bold for his own good—the sort of man who'd never be willing to go for an easy win at mahjong but would insist on building elaborate hands to crush the other players. Still, that wasn't a huge flaw; he might be able to pull off a major win and then retire. His other fault was scrimping, so as to leave as much money as possible for his siblings, especially Third Brother, who had polio and could never marry; if not for this, Mingqi wouldn't even be contemplating marriage himself.

When she thought about it, this wasn't really a problem. He was stingy only toward outsiders, and all the money he put aside went to family—which she would be, if they got married. As she turned this over in her mind, Yafeng felt her future growing clearer. In twenty-three years of life, she'd never once defeated her father. Yachun was the eldest daughter, which gave her some authority. Xuguang was the only son and automatically beloved. As for her, she was stuck in the middle, superfluous. Unexpectedly, this Li Mingqi she'd brought home had routed her father in a single afternoon. Now her big sister was leaving for Jinzhou, and Xuguang didn't care about anything; plus there were dorms at his factory, so she and Mingqi could move in here and more or less rule the roost. At this thought, Gao Yafeng felt her cares floating away.

4

I sat on Second Aunt's bed as she told me the story of my uncle and cousin, and recalled the two funerals my mother had mentioned the night before. The more recent one was my father's, which about thirty people attended. During the ceremony, they played "Moon Reflected in the Second Spring" through scratchy speakers. Ma was completely worn out, so she stayed home while I stood next to Aunt Yachun, shaking everyone's hand. My father, Gao Xuguang, ended up working at the tractor factory. He was fifty when he died. Pancreatic cancer. By the time they caught it, he was already unable to eat, and two months after that he was gone. Apart from the

last week, he was very lucid during those final two months—
fully aware that you can't buck your fate and that his number
was up. He hated traveling, so forget about one last round-
the-world trip, and he'd only ever been loved by my mother,
so there were no old flames to wax nostalgic about. His only
hobby was reading—piles of books covered the bed and
floor. It was strange for a laborer to enjoy reading, especially
a laborer at death's door. From his sickbed, Pa instructed me
to buy some hardbacks, including an out-of-print series called
One Hundred Thousand Whys, which I ordered secondhand.
He said he'd loved these reference books as a child but could
never get the money together to buy them. Now that they
were finally in his possession, he got tired after reading just
a few pages. He didn't have many friends, and hardly anyone
came to see him after he got sick. It was very peaceful. He
spent his waking hours reading, dozing off periodically.

My mother was extremely displeased with his behavior. She
thought he ought to have a bellyful of words for her, long-held
secrets and memories she could cherish. But he had nothing.
In my father's whole life, he'd only ever worked in one place,
and his business trips only ever took him to one destination.
He would get home each day and make dinner, then sink into
a book. When he was away on business, he'd call home at six
every evening, before settling onto the kang of whichever village home he was staying in to read. After he lost his job, he
sold tea eggs in the square, again always in one spot; then he'd
fold up his stall, come home to make dinner, and return to
reading. When he realized he was going, he called my mother
into the sickroom for a private conversation. As far as Ma
remembered afterward, they didn't talk about very much, just
that she should take good care of my grandma after he was

gone. Grandma was quite confused by then, so she wouldn't need to know about his death—they could get away with telling her he was on a work trip. He also urged my mother to remarry, and not to feel she was letting him down—it was enough that they'd shared a harmonious life. His final request was that they play Abing's rendition of his favorite song at his funeral and bury his ashes next to his father's.

Next, he called me into the room to tell me three things. One: I should study hard and get a master's after my bachelor's, then a PhD after that—basically, just keep studying; that was his long-standing wish for me. I could borrow the tuition fees from Aunt Yachun and pay her back when I'd found a job— he'd already consulted her. Two: if Aunt Yafeng's husband, Li Mingqi, ever asked me for anything, I should comply—he was an extraordinary person; it was just bad luck that prevented him from flourishing, and one day he would surely fulfill his potential. The third thing was more of a sigh. He'd spoken quite a bit by then and was exhausted.

—Xiaofeng, there's something I once read in a book, but I didn't really feel it till today.

—What's that, Pa?

—Living your life isn't just a stroll through a field. I can't remember who said that, but now that I think of it, it makes sense. I miss lying on the roof and reading—you should try it if you get the chance.

With that, he shut his eyes, drifted off, and never woke up again.

As far back as I can remember, Li Mingqi seldom came by our home, so he probably didn't have much interaction with my father. During our New Year dinners, it was usually Li Mingqi talking and Pa listening—I never saw any deeper conversation. I found it a little peculiar that he would bring up Li Mingqi at this moment.

My grandfather Gao Likuan died in the 1990s. I was only in my teens then, and my memory is a bit hazy. All I remember is my mother showing up at school and calling me out of class to tell me that he had passed and that we should go weep for him. I was a bit nervous before going into his sickroom, in case I wasn't able to cry. Ma had promised to buy me a water pistol after we were done, giving me an incentive. I went in and found him covered in a white sheet, which was so startling I burst into tears. Grandma was sitting on the edge of the bed, enumerating her late husband's faults—I'd never heard her speak so much. Grandpa had been ill for a decade, after a cerebral hemorrhage brought on by excessive drinking left him bedridden. He was able to speak at first—once in elementary school, I was losing a fight when he saw me from his sickbed and began loudly instructing me through the window about how to hit back. His tactics were effective, and my opponent was soon sprawled on the ground. Later on, Grandpa's Japanese house got torn down in the clearances, so he and Grandma moved in with Second Aunt. Once he'd settled into the apartment she'd been allocated, he could no longer speak, just grunt. He was such an impatient person that when people didn't know what he meant, he would get so worked up he'd almost roll out of bed. His best friend was Uncle Li Mingqi, who turned him over for a sponge bath every day, and who was the only one who could understand the sounds he made. They slept in the same room, and in all those years, Grandpa never got a single bedsore. According to my mother, after Uncle Mingqi's business failed, he was in the middle of gassing himself when he heard Grandpa grunting that he needed to pee. He went to help Grandpa, hugged him and wept for a while, and then decided to go on living. Right before he died, Grandpa summoned his children. He had no savings, but he had received compensation for his house, which they would decide on that day how to divide. Through the whole meeting, his eyes were fixed on his favorite son-in-law, and everyone understood there would be no division—he intended to give everything to Li Mingqi. As a result, Ma and Second Aunt had a big argument and didn't speak for six months.

After Grandpa died, Grandma decided she couldn't stand living with Second Aunt and Uncle Mingqi, who constantly bickered, and moved into our house. At least things were quiet here—Grandma seldom spoke, just like Pa. But Grandma started to forget things. She often forgot to lock the door when she went out to the market, and she burned holes in quite a few woks. Gradually, she was becoming a burden. One of my father's last wishes had been not to tell Grandma about his passing, but Eldest Aunt insisted nonetheless; she reckoned Grandma had a right to know. So Grandma heard the news, and by that evening she had gone deaf. She never recovered her hearing. As for Pa's other wish, that I should study my way to an advanced degree, I didn't manage that, either. After I got my bachelor's, I refused to carry on—I couldn't stand it any longer. Instead, I got a job at a bank, feeling guilty the whole time. Ma remained single and never showed the slightest sign of wanting to remarry. An old classmate got in touch with her, but she screamed at him and pulled the phone cable out of the wall. Li Mingqi never asked me for help, either. Now he'd gone missing and I was looking for him—in a weird way, one of my father's wishes was finally coming true. That hadn't occurred to me during Eldest Aunt's phone call or when Ma got upset with me the night before, but now that I thought of it, there did seem to be a point to my return.

Second Aunt had started flipping through a photo album. She pointed at one picture and said, You were seven. I was a bit surprised that she had a photo of me, but I took a closer look, and sure enough, it was me, wearing a padded coat made by Grandma, sitting on a giant carp, with someone's ass poking out from under the fish.

—Aunt, whose butt is that?

—That's your cousin. Li Gang was always fond of you, since you were kids—he was afraid you'd fall, so he climbed into the fish belly to hold you up.

I thought back but couldn't recall my cousin's fondness. We fought a lot in our youth, and I was always the one getting beaten up. I confessed this, and Aunt Yafeng replied, Your cousin envied you. You're the eldest Gao grandson, and you got into university, while he struggled with his studies. Besides, I was always at war with your uncle, and I never won, so I turned around and hit your cousin, who went out and hit other people. At the end of the day, it's all your uncle's fault.

It was true that I'd rarely seen my cousin since we'd grown up. Apart from his abuse, my other recollection was his talent at snooker. In fact, for a time he'd made his living from it, taking part in all sorts of competitions, though he never reached the level of someone like Ding Junhui; he just played for money in snooker halls. He'd start out acting the fool, striking weird poses and sticking his ass out at weird angles. If anyone took him on, he'd sink ball after ball as if by chance, and since they'd bet money, he'd rake it in late into the night. Afterward, he'd take my hand and we'd walk along past the rows of streetlamps, him humming with his cue over his shoulder. Sometimes he'd lift me up with one arm and say, I'd like to sell you off. I'd ask, Sell me to who? And he'd reply, I haven't decided yet, but someone in the mountains so you'll never taste steamed buns again, somewhere with no roads or electricity; they'll tie a rope to you and make you pull a grindstone. I wouldn't have minded the rest, but no electricity meant I wouldn't be able to watch my cartoons.

Later on, he gave up playing snooker and went off to Guangdong to smuggle motorbikes. Not knowing how things worked over there, he got the door slammed on him before he could stick a foot in—a local gang leader had him tossed into the sea. He managed to climb to shore and slink back to Shenyang. Second Aunt said:

—I'm not sure what your cousin's been up to recently; I think he's helping people collect debts.

—He's even skinnier than me. How's he going to do that?

She laughed. —It's not about size—he's had a couple of dragons tattooed on his arms, call it an investment. Listen, your cousin might not have gotten as far in school as you, but he's smart—someone was coming after him for money he owed, and he thought, If you can't beat them, why not join them? So he joined forces with the loan sharks, and now the hunted has become the hunter.

—So is he missing or not?

—He's not answering his phone, and he hasn't been home for a week, not since he showed up with a huge load of steamed buns. Look, it doesn't really matter whether you find your uncle or not. I've got his pension book here, so he can live or die as far as I'm concerned; I'll be able to repay his debts eventually. But I need Li Gang to come home—he has depression.

—How did my cousin get a high-class sickness like that?

—Who knows? Collecting money is stressful: you have to please your bosses, and debtors are as sneaky as rabbits. A few weeks ago he was helping with some evictions, and a resident who didn't want to move almost broke his leg. Your cousin's been talking about buying a house, and that's probably putting more pressure on him.

—Why's he buying a house?

—You've spent too long at school, child, it's made your brain soft. Your cousin is thirty-six now, why would he wait any longer to get married?

—Does he have a girlfriend?

—Never seen one, but I bet he does, otherwise why would he need a house? That's called deduction.

—So, Sherlock Holmes, where should I look for him?

—Across Xinhua Road, there's a place called Mynah Snooker Hall at the corner. He was always playing there—go in and ask. If only I could get down the stairs, I'd have dragged that bastard back home long ago.

—He's still playing snooker?

—Used to be a career, but now it's just for fun. Careers earn money, and fun costs money, understand?

—Make sure to stay off the phone—I'll call you if I learn anything.

Second Aunt walked me to the door.

—I heard that having depression means you might jump off a building, so if you see your cousin, tell him to wait till after I'm dead. If he jumps now, no one's going to give him a funeral, and he'll be stuck chilling in the morgue.

She shut the door behind me, and I heard her slippers shuffling slowly away.

Mynah Snooker Hall wasn't large, just a dozen tables or so, but the lighting was soft and pleasantly warm, like springtime. There weren't many people around, and beneath the lights, the neat triangles of balls looked like precious artifacts in a museum display. The boss sat playing mahjong on a stark white Apple iMac. When he noticed me looking around, he stood up.

—Can I help you?

—I'm looking for someone called Li Gang. Thirties, skinny, arm tattoos.

—Gang-san hasn't been in for a while. You looking for a game? He doesn't play professionally anymore.

—He's my cousin, I need to talk to him.

He pointed at a girl on the nearby couch. —You should ask Mireiko. Mireiko, play with this guy for a while.

This was unexpected, meeting a Japanese girl in a place like this. Mireiko was in her early twenties and had on a dress and silky stockings. She put her rhinestone-encrusted phone on the edge of the table, fetched a cue from the cabinet, and said, Do you have your own cue? Her voice was pure Shenyang, the accent even stronger than my own.

—I don't play; I'm looking for Li Gang.

—Go get one from over there. It's eighty yuan a frame; we'll start with three.

I had no choice but to obey. She let me go first, and I screwed it up.

—Don't grip too hard—you'll splinter the cue, and the ball won't go any faster. Let your arm do the work; your shoulder is an axle.

I tried again and managed a decent break.

—So you're not Japanese?

—*You're* Japanese. It's a stage name.

—Li Gang is my cousin. He hasn't been home for a week. I came from Beijing to look for him. I have to find him quick so I can get back to my job.

—You think Beijing's so important? What matters more, your cousin or your job? Sink a long shot and I'll answer your questions.

I tried, but I began sweating profusely and couldn't hit the ball in. She gave me a few more pointers: for instance, it helped when I focused my eyes elsewhere, making the ball a white blur. My glasses kept sliding down my nose, until she took them off and put them on the bar. Finally, the ball teetered on the edge of the hole and tumbled in.

—Good, now pay up.

I handed her the cash, and she slipped it into her stocking top.

—Your cousin's sick. This money will buy him medicine. Prozac. Now, hurry back to your job in Beijing. It's not like he's your brother. Just say you couldn't find him—no one will blame you.

I put my glasses back on.

—Never mind getting back to work. You asked me which was more important. I've thought about it, and it's my cousin. I have to see him. We can talk later about whether or not he's going home.

—You must be Xiaofeng.

—I am.

—Your cousin says you're the only person in your family who isn't useless. But you're blind as soon as you take your glasses off—that seems pretty useless to me.

—It's true. I've been to university, but my life is still a mess. Everything they say about my success is made up, but every family needs one fake person to be proud of.

She glanced at me. Shrugging on her coat, she drew a hundred yuan from her stocking and gave it to the boss.

—Your share, Mynah. I'm taking the afternoon off. I might be back later—we'll see.

Mireiko's cramped two-bedroom was near my aunt's place, maybe a thousand meters in a straight line. She led me in, and there was my cousin on the couch watching TV, skinny as ever, with a bandage around his neck. Next to him sat a girl, whom Mireiko introduced as Nanako.

Nanako spat out a melon seed shell and smiled at me. My cousin raised his eyes.

—Xiaofeng?

—Hey, give your mother a call. I don't care whether you're depressed or you're hiding from debts—do it now.

- -Aren't you supposed to be in Beijing?

—Eldest Aunt asked me to look for you and Uncle Mingqi.

- -You came all the way just for me?

—Yes, just for you

—Come here.

He patted the sofa. I walked over and sat down next to him.

5

After the two men had drained the last drop of liquor, Gao Likuan climbed down from the kang. It was one in the morning. His daughters were snoozing with their heads together against the edge of the platform. About two-thirds done, Yachun's sweater rested in the kang drawer, knitting needles sticking out. Yafeng hadn't managed to expel her bellyful of words, and now she was dreaming about dancing with a spirited man, who upon closer examination turned out to be the handsome lead actor from *Taking Tiger Mountain by Strategy*. Zhao Suying was sitting on a bench and leaning against the cool stove—she'd fallen asleep listening to the radio. Beforehand, she'd managed to climb up onto the roof to drape a light rug over Xuguang. As soon as Gao's feet touched the floor, he almost fell flat on his face. He said, Come on, I'll teach you qinggong. Mingqi was nine-tenths of the way to wasted, but with the conversation flowing, he didn't feel the least bit tired. He followed Gao into the courtyard. Gao gestured at the ladder and said, Go on, I'll follow behind. The first lesson is falling to the ground without a sound. Halfway up, Mingqi turned to Gao.

—Mentor, I hadn't finished talking earlier—I do have an ambition.

—What's that?

—The parachutes are just a starting point. I want to build a flying device.

—A what?

—A flying device. Something you can put on like clothes, to fly you higher than the roof. Say you want to visit my family—just slip it on, glide above the street, and land in our courtyard. Then you come right in and start drinking.

—What would it run on?

—I was thinking diesel, but that's too heavy. I need to do more research. Maybe a battery?

—What size battery?

—Specially made. Rechargeable, ideally. Enough to take you a few kilometers on one charge.

Gao nodded. —If Lin Biao had had a gadget like that, there's no telling how far he'd have gotten.

—This device won't get you too far. If people were able to fly out of the country just like that, there would be chaos. Everything has to start with baby steps. A while back, I heard on the radio that almost every household in America has a car. Now they have gridlock in some cities. So could we. America took a winding road to get where they are, but with my device we'll pass right over their heads.

—That's profound. Your head doesn't look too big, but your brain is huge, it's got to be a couple pounds heavier than mine.

—Inventions like this need capital. The higher-ups didn't go for it—they said my brain had worms. Will you help me? I'll pay you back. Everyone who invests gets to be a part owner. In time, you won't just be my father-in-law, you'll also be my boss.

Gao batted that away. —I don't want to be your boss, just your father-in-law. I'll lend you the money; I'd only piss it away on booze otherwise. Just do it, and answer to no one but yourself. When you're done, each member of our families will use one. We'll fly around and show off in front of the neighbors.

Mingqi was moved. —Sir, when you're old and no one wants to take care of you, I will. But you can't go back on your word just because you're drunk.

—We've only just met for the first time, so we don't understand each other yet. I'm Gao Likuan, and my word is my word when I'm drunk—it's only when I'm sober that nothing I say counts. Now go on up to the roof, I need to take a piss.

By the time Gao was done, he'd forgotten all about Mingqi up above, waiting to learn qinggong. He went back into the room, stretched his legs out under the table, shut his lone eye, and started snoring. Mingqi sat on the roof for a while, and when Gao didn't show up, he started considering his own affairs. He felt a little guilty—he didn't hate Gao Yafeng, but he didn't particularly like her, either. She was ordinary—or, to put it harshly, a bit vulgar, her thoughts no deeper than those of anyone you picked off the street at random. She was hardworking and tidy but also talkative, and there wouldn't be much silence once they were married. The thought made his throat tighten, and he wanted to be sick. He tried retching, but nothing came out. He'd started seeing Yafeng because of her situation: she hadn't been sent down to the countryside, so she'd been able to work for quite a while, and her profession was a good one: she was a mechanic. As the rhyme goes: *Mechanic, miller, lathe-hand, best jobs in the land.* Her wages were double his, and she wasn't saddled with too many siblings; it was just the three of them. Both her parents were long-standing workers with impeccable backgrounds, so their earnings were above average. They could feel secure in everything they did, from getting involved with politics to buying apples at Tiexi Department Store. Gao Likuan had a reputation for not caring about anything or anyone, and Mingqi had been nervous before coming here today, but after their conversation, he felt much safer. No wonder his father always used to say, Mentor Gao has all kinds of faults, but one good thing about him: there's no wickedness in his heart.

He recalled his father's last words. Apart from his advice about being a Napoleon, he'd also said, If the day comes when you don't know where your next meal is coming from, no need to go far, just take your brothers and sisters to Gao Likuan's front door; he'll make sure you don't starve. His father had been a shrewd judge of character—I can see this patch of ground, thought Mingqi, but he could see past the horizon. A shame he couldn't see far enough into the future to know that he only had to hang on for a few more years, and the troubles would come to an end. There was no need to despair like that, no need to be so selfish, to throw up his hands and walk away, leaving so many people behind to burden Mingqi. He remembered his father's appearance, the white undershirt he wore around the house, how he'd made Mingqi a kite, his deft hands that could do whatever they set out to, sitting at the desk writing his instructions with his fountain pen, ripping the paper up and starting again when he got a single word wrong, and finally he remembered his father hanging from the rafters, like a dead chicken, dead weight—no matter how hard Mingqi tried, he couldn't get him down. At this thought, he had to dab the tears off his cheeks and dry his fingers on his shirt.

Something clattered on the roof tiles and woke Gao Xuguang. Out of the corner of his eye, he saw Li Mingqi. How odd: Xuguang was usually the only one who enjoyed hanging out on the roof. Murky black filled Xuguang's field of vision. There were no stars, and he couldn't see the moon, either, just unending darkness rising above him. It was much cooler at night. Now and then a gust of wind lifted a corner of the light rug that covered him, and it felt as if the dark were speaking to him, though he didn't understand its language. Lower down, he saw rooftops and elm trees. All the lights were out, except for a lone streetlamp in the distance by someone's gatepost. This sight was familiar to Xuguang—in fact, he'd been waiting for it. Sometimes he wondered what this tangle of people who made up his family were busying themselves for every day, or why they found so many topics worthy of discussion, argument, insistence, compromise, why they became happy or sad, why they got angry and then forgave. He had no idea why fate had seen fit to take Gao Likuan, Zhao Suying, Gao Yachun, Gao Yafeng, himself, and now this Li Mingqi and put them all together in this era, in this place, and leave them to their own devices. Why were these the people he had to face every day, who affected every aspect of his life? Why not a bunch of Americans instead, or Soviets, or Eskimos, or alien beings? His heart and mind would never be completely aligned with theirs; he would never be able to immerse himself in the things they cared about. Most of the time, he just found them noisy. He enjoyed reading, but he didn't plan to take the university entrance exam. Only Gao Likuan thought it didn't matter whether he studied or not. Everyone else gave him a hard time about his decision. A scholar needs to become a college student, just as a horse ought to have shoes nailed to its hooves. But that wasn't how Xuguang thought. He had a few considerations, not that he'd shared them with anyone. First of all, taking the entrance exam had its risks—not the embarrassment of failure but the danger of acceptance. His eldest sister would soon be leaving, and if Xuguang was sent far away, his mother's life might turn into nothing but suffering. Xuguang had once thought of how he hadn't killed a single person during the Cultural Revolution, hadn't even taken to the streets during the violent struggles—but if he wasn't around to prevent it, his dad might do something to his mother that only murder could avenge. Second, if he became a college student, that would make him some kind of professional egghead, and to what end? Look at the ten years that had just gone by, and project them forward two decades—would these college students enjoy the fruits of their labors? He'd witnessed a classmate slitting a teacher's nose, and if he'd wanted, he could have grabbed the knife and slashed that teacher's cheek as well. They said A one day and B the next, and now the university entrance exams were back, but who could say that they wouldn't turn from B back to A again? All that studying, only to end up as a stinking ninth-rate intellectual? He didn't know who came up with that phrase, stinking ninth-rate intellectual, and though Xuguang loved knowledge, he had to admit that intellectuals did indeed give off a stench. Third, starting this year, he'd gotten very close to Ling, a woman on his production team. She was pure as sunlight, and never questioned his silence and melancholy. If he absolutely had to spend the rest of his life with one person, this girl would suffice. That's what married life was to him. Being alone would be best of all, but going insane wasn't good. Of course, he might go insane through marriage, but that would be a socially meaningful form of madness, more like despair or disappointment, rather than the shattering of his very soul. Besides, his mother was hoping for this to happen, and perhaps that was her only wish, that there could be a third generation in the Gao clan, particularly a grandson. There was one other point Xuguang himself hadn't been willing to acknowledge. Over the last decade, chaotic reality had so numbed his brain that he no longer felt much of anything, and he wasn't inclined to make any major changes that might send his life careening down a perilous road to the mere possibility of hope.

Li Mingqi wiped away his tears and stood up, startling Xuguang again. Having missed the conversation in the house,

Xuguang assumed Mingqi had flounced up here in a fit of pique. Actually, though, the only things urging Mingqi on were the Western Phoenix liquor in his belly and his blazing dreams. He wanted to give a speech, but he didn't know what to say. He waved his arms and turned his wrist like he was scooping rice into a bowl, as if that might bring the words from his belly out into the air. The main thing is the battery, he said after a while. The battery has to be light but also powerful— the theory of fluid mechanics isn't difficult, we're surrounded by air currents, and that's what will propel us up into the sky. He belched, then went on. No need to fly too high; as long as your toes float above other people's heads, that's enough. Our streets will be three-dimensional—you know? Second-story windows will become doors, and department stores can convert all their windows into shop counters. You want two pounds of freeze-dried pears? Sure! Hand over your money, hang the bag of pears on your arm, and off you fly. Think about it—if a human being could hover three to five meters above the ground, cleaning the outside of your house would be a breeze, and even getting rid of sparrows wouldn't be difficult—you could just swipe them all away with ease. Lovers would no longer need to find groves of trees for privacy, since they could just soar upward. Unfortunately, girls will have to stop wearing skirts. One other problem: in the stratosphere, little force is needed, but at low heights, you'll have to keep blasting air downward to stay aloft, as if you're farting down on people from above.

Hearing this, Gao Xuguang was delighted. Mingqi hadn't just spoken these words, he'd acted them out. Freeze-dried pears? Sure! Then he'd mimed handing over the cash, receiving two pounds of fruit. One moment he embodied a panicked sparrow, the next a girl clutching at her skirt, and finally a pedestrian assailed by flatulence. A wave crested in Xuguang's heart. This Li Mingqi was different from anyone else he knew. His acquaintances worried that they would stumble and fall just walking down the street, while this guy dreamed of soaring through the sky.

Xuguang let Mingqi's imaginary scenario run through his mind. If this flying device were a success, first of all it would save him from having to clamber up the ladder every time he wanted to read on the roof. Next, he'd get one for his mother, so whenever Gao Likuan turned violent, she could jump into the air and fly away. But if his mother could buy one, then so could his father. Still, she was small and thin, so she'd be able to fly faster, and even if they went at the same speed, Gao's battery would run out first and he'd tumble back down to earth.

Xuguang thought about utopian socialism, about Robert Owen, Henri de Saint-Simon, Charles Fourier. Forget Owen, but Saint-Simon and Fourier were such beautiful, airy names, perfectly suited to the soaring dreams of socialism itself. This aeronaut Li Mingqi's name might not be as grand, but his ruminations touched the same realm. Xuguang didn't conclude from this that Mingqi would fail; quite the opposite— Marxism derived from utopian socialism, Chairman Mao's thought derived from Marxism, and so forth. In other words, everything had a source, and though sometimes the source was shabby and lowborn, that didn't determine the outcome, which could be mighty. The famous mathematician Chen Jingrun had researched why one plus one equals two, and from that simple question, he had reached a profound conclusion: the theorem that bears his name. That's an exceptional

person. We all add one and one every day but never consider
why counting has to happen like this. We all walk down the
street every day and never imagine our feet leaving the ground
to glide over the rooftops. The more Xuguang thought along
these lines, the more he believed humanity's great break-
throughs all had their beginnings in moments like this, Li
Mingqi's drunken gesturing. Xuguang didn't drink, nor had
he experienced the heady drug of ambition, but as he witnessed
Mingqi in this state, a certain happiness rubbed off on him.
The numb portion of Xuguang's brain flashed suddenly, then
extinguished itself like the night before him, and a moment
later he was asleep again, the nocturnal breeze ruffling his
hair and tugging at his stiff shirt collar. Still, the epiphany left
its mark. For the rest of his life, no matter what Mingqi did,
Xuguang never changed his opinion: Li Mingqi was extraordinary.

Mingqi didn't realize that he'd had an audience. Worn
out from speechifying, he sat down, his whirring mind still
pondering the many questions that remained about the flying device's usage. If everyone was up in the air, would we
need traffic rules there, too? Should we affix lights to our rears?
Otherwise, you might find yourself tailgating, if you weren't
paying attention. And where should traffic lights go? Should
poles extend dozens of meters high? How many lanes could
the sky provide? If you were drunk and the wind blew on
you, would the volume of liquor in your belly feel like it had
doubled? Suddenly Mingqi felt queasy, and he slowly climbed
down the ladder.

Back inside, he saw Zhao Suying with her head resting on
the stove, apron still wrapped around her, sound asleep. He
called out quietly, Auntie? She didn't respond, but he could

hear her snoring very quietly. He turned off the radio, reached out to cradle her face, carried her over to the kang, and laid her next to Gao. She rolled over but didn't wake up. Gao was snoring like a tractor. Zhao Suying huddled by his side like a dog. Yachun and Yafeng were still leaning against the foot of the kang. Mingqi stood for a while, gazing at Yafeng. He'd never seen her asleep before. She neither snored nor ground her teeth; she was smiling merrily, and there was a sheen of sweat on her brow. Her nose twitched. Yafeng was more adorable asleep than awake. She looked tiny and peaceful. He watched her for a while, then noticed the almost-finished sweater in the kang drawer. Mingqi had secretly knitted all his eight siblings' woolen clothing—it always felt a little off to him, a grown man knitting. At this moment, though, hot blood was still pumping through his body, and his hands were restless. Sitting on the bench, he began working swiftly, and by dawn the sweater was done. He even varied the patterns on the sleeves. Restoring the finished garment to the kang cabinet, he stood up and walked back out.

The sun wasn't visible yet, and the moonlight hadn't entirely faded, leaving a faint wash of pale blue. He was a little weary. This had been his first visit to the hutong, and now it felt utterly unfamiliar, but he thought he'd be able to find his way out. He hopped onto his bicycle, one foot on a pedal and the other pushing off the ground, and set out for work as usual.

6

Neither Mireiko nor Nanako was dating my cousin. His girlfriend sold cosmetics in Zhongxing Mall. These two were just his friends. After Li Gang fell ill, they worried that he would die, so they brought him to their house. One watched him by day, the other by night. These shifts worked perfectly: Mireiko's main job was accompanying players at the snooker hall, and her side gig was assisting guests in the karaoke lounge; for Nanako, it was the other way around. They both gave up their second jobs to keep an eye on my cousin around the clock. Why had his illness flared up? The cosmetics sales-girl had demanded that he buy an apartment, and she'd gen-erously given him a six-month deadline. She said, It doesn't matter what job you have, as long as you can get hold of a hundred-square-meter apartment within the city limits; then my parents will even find your tattoos attractive. Since my cousin only had the tattoos and not an apartment, he went hat in hand to his friends. Those hooligans knew he was just as powerless as they were to repay any debt—so despite all the time they'd spent hanging out and having fun, as soon as word spread that he needed to borrow money, they all became incredibly busy. My cousin then thought of loan sharks—since, after all, that was his own line of work—but what could he offer as collateral? Then it occurred to him: the deed to his ma's place. This wasn't easy, because Aunt Yafeng kept the deed well hidden, not from my cousin but from her husband, who'd spent decades trying to get his hands on it. Back then, she and Uncle Mingqi were always fighting over money, and when she didn't give in to his demands for cash, they'd turn to violence. Huddling in a corner, my cousin saw his father grab a cleaver and his mother a paring knife. The cleaver sliced through the air, though Uncle Mingqi didn't actually want to kill his wife—he'd have been hauled in front of the firing squad if he'd succeeded. Besides, she was Gao Likuan's daughter, and he couldn't insult Gao by hacking her to death. Anyway, he didn't know where the valuables were hidden. For her part, Second Aunt really did want to kill her husband. There was no middle ground to her emotions, and only a thin line separated love and murder. From dancing, Uncle Mingqi was light on his feet, and so he managed to avoid being stabbed, but he never got his hands on the deed or her savings.

My cousin waited till Second Aunt was asleep to ransack the house. When he came upon a pair of dungarees he'd worn when he was six, he thought, How odd that she's hung on to them—don't they look much smaller, like a rag doll's. He picked them up and felt the stiff pocket—something good was in there. He ripped it open to find the savings book and the apartment deed. He didn't have the PIN for the savings book, so he just took the document, stuffed in a few real estate leaflets to make up the bulk, and sewed everything together again. With the deed as collateral, he easily secured a loan for the deposit on an apartment. Unfortunately, he was a few days late. The cosmetics-counter girl was very punctual—she was practically German in this regard—and as soon as the deadline passed, she took up with an old classmate from junior high, a Mazda salesman, whom she must have been keeping in reserve for some time. Perhaps she'd always had a spare, and this whole thing about buying an apartment was just a charade. My cousin rushed over with a knife to start a fight, but he found some gang members waiting to beat him up. He walked home with his tail between his legs. The more he thought about it, the more frustrated he got, until finally he slashed his own throat. Once you lose, though, you tend to keep losing, and he didn't even manage to kill himself.

Mireiko and Nanako kept interrupting each other as they

told the story. My cousin just sat, listening and smiling, but
didn't try to butt in, and he certainly didn't contradict them.
I believed that he had depression—he wasn't playing around;
he actually was ill. His smile was a classic depressive's smile, a
melancholy grin, as if nothing mattered. Mireiko said to him,
Look, your cousin's here, why don't you talk to him? You'll rot
your brain, watching TV all day. Nanako said, We've been so
busy standing guard over you, we haven't had the chance to
go shopping for ages. Your cousin's here, so we're going out,
and you can fend for yourself. The two girls discussed their
destination, readied themselves, and set off.

It was suddenly very quiet in the room—nothing but the
gunfire from the TV, *rat-tat-tat*. My cousin leaned toward me
and said, I talk softly now, come closer. His voice was gravelly
from his neck injury, like a radio with a bad signal. He asked
about my life and job, and I gave him a quick summary: no
girlfriend, working at a bank, waking up at six every morning,
a two-hour subway ride to the office, then another two-hour
ride back, getting home so exhausted that my head no sooner
touched the pillow than I fell asleep. He asked what I did in
the bank, and I told him roughly. He asked for more details,
and I realized he was very familiar with banking operations,
apart from some jargon that I needed to explain. Then I understood: the debt-collection agencies he assisted must operate
along similar principles. We kept chatting. My cousin asked:

—Have you been to see Grandma recently?

—No.

—When you're done here, you should go and see her.

—Mm.

—What do you mean, Mm? She misses you, did you know
that?

—She's not in her right mind, is she?

—She keeps calling me. She's confused about now, but she remembers the past clearly.

—She calls you?

—Yes, on my cell phone. Almost every month. Look, when Grandpa and Grandma were living with us, my parents never stopped working, and there were times when my father didn't come home at all. Grandpa just lay in bed, so Grandma and I became good friends.

—That can't be right. Grandma's deaf. How would she call you?

—Her ears are sharper than mine. If she didn't pretend to be deaf, would she have had any peace, these past few years? After your father died, she stopped wanting to talk, and she didn't like hearing other people talk, either.

—So what does she talk about on the phone?

—Everything. She talks about the past, Grandpa, Grandpa's apprentice, Aunt Yachun, my ma, your pa, my pa, and you.

—What does she say about me?

—When you were small, she would give you money from her handkerchief to buy candy, and you complained because she only gave you a little at a time. She still has that hand-kerchief, and she'd like to buy you more candy, but you don't want it now. She wishes she'd died before your father, so she'd have had a son to see her off, and also as a little boy you'd have cried more for her.

I was silent for a while.

—Why doesn't Grandma want to call me?

—She knows you've made something of yourself and your time is precious. She doesn't want to bother you. And there's one other thing.

—What?

—Grandma loves you most of all, but she's friends with me, and you tell your friends what's in your heart.

—What do you say to her?

—I tell her that I'm doing well, that I'm about to get married. I say she should come and celebrate with us, and in a couple of years she'll be a great-grandma.

I was silent again.

—Do you know where my uncle is?

—Yes.

—Can you make him go home?

—He's not going back.

My cousin stood up, went into the inner room, and came back with the title deed.

—I got someone to help me sell off my new apartment, then I paid off the loan and regained the deed. Give it to my ma.

I took it from him. —You're not going back either?

—I'm not going back either.

The film had ended, and the TV was now showing an ad for a sporting goods brand that apparently was used by Africans, Europeans, Latin Americans, refugees, rich people, and disabled people. My cousin stared at the screen for a while.

—Did you know your uncle made a flying device?

—A flying device?

—A sort of backpack that carries you up into the sky. He called it the portable flying machine.

—No, I didn't know that.

—It didn't work out. Fuck, how could it ever have succeeded? Your pa helped him get the parts.

—My pa?

—Yes, your father, my uncle. He stole the parts from his factory.

—Since when was Pa that bold?

—Aunt Yachun lent him money too, for his machine. I don't know why, but the whole family believed he could pull it off. After he failed, he tried his hand at all kinds of businesses: he sold coal, he opened a restaurant, he dealt tobacco in Yunnan, he raised ants for Yilishen.

—Raised ants?

—He filled my room with their little boxes. I slept on the floor. Sometimes the ants escaped, climbed over my face, and bit me. Later on he gave dance lessons, sold Nutrilite supplements for Amway, all kinds of little things. I'm very proud of him—he, too, believed all along that he'd succeed eventually. He once told me that knowledge is strength. Though that's just half the saying.

—What's the other half?

—Labor creates freedom. He told me about an old lady somewhere who went to college at seventy and started a business aged eighty. He thought it was never too late.

I nodded. —I don't know what the right thing to do is, but I feel I ought to see Uncle Mingqi at least once. Whether or not he goes back, at least I could set eyes on him and give a proper report when I return.

—You'll see him. You'll see him tonight. We're family, and no matter what, our fates are closely linked. I didn't do anything today. Those two girls were watching me, and I couldn't have gone anywhere. But you're here now, and so we can go out tonight.

For the next few hours, he didn't say a word. The TV started playing another movie, a comedy, and he watched it with rapt interest, though he didn't laugh. The main character turned into God and could walk on water, staring in shocked delight at his own feet, wondering why they didn't sink.

The sky blackened. In a northeastern winter, everything gets dark by six. The cold seeped in through the window cracks, like cruel words. My cousin didn't turn on the lights. Finally, the movie ended. The credits rolled and music played. My cousin stood up and got dressed. Come on, he said.

From the drawer, he took a gleaming gold watch and put it on. We went downstairs, into Mynah Snooker Hall. The boss said, You're here? He said, I am, could I have my cue? The boss went behind the bar and emerged with a pale yellow stick with a dark brown grip, like a beam of light. My cousin said, Play with me? The boss went into a storeroom at the back of the shop and came out with a cue of his own. They started shooting. A few others gathered to watch, cheering them on. One by one, they drifted away, until it was just the three of us. The two of them kept going till eleven at night. Finally, my cousin stopped.

—We've been playing together for twenty years.

—Yes, we have.

—I'm leaving.

—Do you want to take the cue with you?

—Sure.

The boss got a black case from behind the bar. My cousin dismantled his cue, placed it in the box, tucked it under his arm, and led the way out.

We went to my aunt's building. The courtyard was pitch-black. My cousin looked up—almost all the windows were dark. He pointed at one of them and said, That's my room. I couldn't tell which one he was pointing at. He said, When I was a kid, I used to look out of that window, and the farthest I could see was this courtyard. Back then, I often thought about running away, but then I'd realize it was safer to stay tucked up in bed. I said, On this trip, I realized I don't dream when I'm sleeping in my old bed at home—I'm always dreaming when I'm away from here.

My cousin nodded. He shouted toward the window, Hey! Where's Li Gang? No one answered, and his voice was swiftly inhaled by the night. He walked out of the courtyard, summoned a taxi, and said to the driver, Take South Fifth Street to Red Flag Square. I said, Is Uncle Mingqi there? He said, Yes, that's where he is. I said, What's he doing there, so late at night? He thought about it but didn't answer.

My memory of Red Flag Square was that it was brightly lit, but that day it was dark. I'm not sure if I'd remembered wrongly, or if I'd never been there at that time of night. The old-fashioned octagonal lamps at the corners were unlit. The marble slabs in the square were shinier and smoother than I'd remembered. Chairman Mao's statue stood dead center, and underneath it was a clump of dark shadows. I looked up at the Chairman's right hand, which was raised aloft. It looked especially friendly in the gloom, an amiable hand that anyone could approach. My cousin said, There used to be pigeons here. I said, Oh, really? He said, That's what I heard; I don't know why they went away, maybe it was the cold. We walked to the other side of the square, and I saw some figures bustling about behind the Chairman's back. As we drew closer, I saw my uncle. He held a hurricane lantern and was directing the others. He looked about the same as I remembered: still handsome, with clearly defined features and deep-set eyes, like a Western devil. His eyelashes were as long as ever. But his face and neck had gotten a little shriveled, and his hair was clearly a wig—you could see bald patches where his sideburns should have been. I heard the sound of an air pump. My uncle spotted me and came over. He was a head taller than me and wore a capacious down coat over white trousers, not a speck of dirt on them, and leather shoes.

—Xiaofeng?

—Uncle Mingqi. Long time no see.

—You're coming, too?

—Coming where? You haven't been home for a while, Uncle—we've all been looking for you.

He smiled. —Surely no one's looking for me. How are you these days? I hear you've done quite well for yourself.

—Not really, I'm just a bank worker.

—How many lines are there on the Beijing subway these days?

I tried to remember. —Maybe a dozen? I'm not sure.

—I've heard one taxi ride in Beijing can cost you fifty yuan?

—Mostly because of the gridlock. You sit there not moving, and the meter ticks away.

—How's your mother?

—Not bad, though she doesn't like going outdoors.

—You tell your mother that I, Li Mingqi, haven't forgotten her. If I hadn't been so busy recently, I'd have gone to see her. It's not easy, being alone. She ought to find a partner quick.

—You'd better tell her yourself; she won't listen to me.

—You pass on the message. You're the head of the household now.

The sound was getting louder, and I saw a balloon swelling up beside Chairman Mao, getting larger and larger, until

it was suspended in midair. A large basket dangled from it.
Uncle Mingqi said:

—Xiaofeng, it's almost dawn, we can't delay any longer.

I remembered what he'd once said, that you had to be a
Napoleon. Even if you ended up imprisoned on an island, at
least you'd have done something with your life. You had to fight
against the current—otherwise, you'd end up on the trash heap.

—What's with the balloon?

—I designed it. Normally, these things don't stay airborne
for too long, but I calculate this model can keep going for a
month. Crucially, it doesn't just have to follow the wind; it can
go straight up. A month from now, we'll have reached South
America.

—South America?

I envisioned giant botanical gardens, women with baskets
on their backs picking bananas.

—Yes, South America.

My cousin slapped me on the shoulder and said, Well, I'll
be off. Take care, and don't forget to give the title deed back
to my mother. With that, he came over, tossed the cue case
into the basket, and reached in for a large backpack. I said,
Hang on, Uncle, you said the balloon could go straight up—
but won't it explode sooner or later? He said, That's right, so
all of us have a parachute. I designed these parachutes thirty
years ago, and though more advanced ones came along, tons
of these are piled up in my warehouse.

A man in a wheelchair waved for my uncle to come over.
Uncle Mingqi said, Listen, kid, being born into this world is
like a parachute jump from wherever we were before, and now
we're preparing to jump one more time, into a new beginning.

As for you, when you go back, tell them you saw us, say we were preparing to go down south to do business. If you're your grandfather's grandson, your father's son, you'll let us do this.

An enormous truck sped past the square, wheels squealing. Uncle Mingqi said, All right, we're off. Stay well, take good care of your mother. As Confucius says, when your parents are around, don't go far—just make your way in Beijing, maybe bring your mother over to live with you.

With that, he scooped up the wheelchair user and deposited him into the basket, then folded the wheelchair and tossed that in, too. I remembered my mother telling me that Uncle Mingqi had a little brother who'd had polio—this was probably him. As if unfettered by gravity, my Uncle Li Mingqi leaped weightlessly into the basket himself. It now held five people, four men and one woman. Apart from my cousin, the others were about my uncle's age. I didn't go any closer—I had no idea what to say—but watched them from a distance. Uncle Mingqi tugged on a cord, and flames began flickering above the basket. The balloon rose, past the Red Guard waving his flag, past Chairman Mao's head, higher and higher, in a perfectly straight line, and then drifted diagonally, until it had vanished into the night, and I could see nothing at all.

I stayed where I was, feeling exhaustion wash over me. I wanted very much to hurry home to sleep.

I stretched out my arm to call a taxi. I don't know how much time passed, but not a single vehicle went by. The road around the square was like a silent river. I felt I might be about to doze off, just standing there on the edge of the square, in the middle of this winter night, slipping away into dreamland.

BRIGHT HALL

1

The lunatic Liao Chenghu once drew a map of Yanfen Street, including the history of most of its buildings. Liao, a toilet cleaner, was thirty years older than me, but we became friends. Decades ago, when the country was in turmoil, he studied sculpture. Probably because he wouldn't let them push him around at the school, he was seen as a troublemaker and sent down to Yanfen Street. Apparently he didn't behave himself here either, and made a reactionary clay statue. The Red Guards arrested him and cut off both middle fingers, so he'd never be able to sculpt again. That's when he lost his mind. Liao's madness surfaced twice during our yearlong friendship, once in winter and once in fall. The winter incident was in 1992, when he crossed the road to the bicycle repair shop just as a passerby was taking a piece of firewood from the shop's stove to thaw a frozen valve. Liao stood with both hands in the sleeves of his black padded jacket, then abruptly said to the passerby, Show me your fingers. Confused, the guy nevertheless did as he was told. Liao said, Ha, I knew it, you've got an extra, then pulled a cleaver from his sleeve, and attacked. The shop owner kicked him to the ground and snatched the knife away. Motherfucker, he yelled, if you come here again, I'll slice off your dick. The following fall, when I was twelve and Liao Chenghu forty-two, we went to Shadow Lake, at the heart of Yanfen Street, to burn offerings for his dead friend. That's when he had his second episode: he lunged at me, fell into the lake, and drowned. It's not a very interesting story, so I won't say any more—my point is that he left behind a map depicting every road, hill, and lake in the Yanfen Street district. The whole thing was meticulously done in fountain pen, a sea of blue.

My father had two sisters—he was the middle child. His big sister got married and moved to Dalian, where she was a nurse. They corresponded occasionally, and after I learned to write, my father dictated his letters to me. These letters were always signed from the whole family, all three of us, and covered inconsequential topics selected with great caution. Eldest Aunt's replies often invited us to spend the New Year with her in Dalian, but we never did, probably because she didn't know that my mother had left—she went on a business trip down south with a coworker and never returned—and because we lacked suitable clothes. But whenever Eldest Aunt sent money, Pa returned it untouched. After he lost his job, he threw himself into drinking and could no longer be bothered to keep up their correspondence, but I could imitate his writing style and carried on answering the letters anyway. Pa never talked about his younger sister, but I knew she existed because Eldest Aunt once wrote that Pa should contact her—she'd heard Youngest

Aunt had moved to Yanfen Street. Pa didn't seem to care that his little sister had come to live very close to us, nor to wonder what had brought her this low.

To make ends meet, Pa sold a cabinet he'd built with his own hands. Next, he carted our black-and-white TV set to Yang Saner's place on the street behind ours and exchanged it for thirty yuan. He'd already paid my school fees at the start of the semester, so at least we didn't have to worry about them for the next few months—but then winter arrived, and he hadn't bought any coal, which made me nervous. This was the second winter after my mother left. The year before, my father had managed to haul in a load of coal, which he stored in the shack in our courtyard. It was low quality, mixed with quite a bit of sand, and our stove produced thick clouds of billowing smoke. Now the first signs of winter were here again—the poplar tree by the crossroads had shed all its leaves, and the bicycle repair shop's owner had fired up his stove. Evenings were difficult. Frost bloomed in the window cracks. Pa wore padded trousers and padded shoes and lounged on the ice-cold kang platform, drinking. The only thing on the table was a white pear, which he carefully cut into pieces, bringing each sliver to his mouth with the knife.

Finally, snow arrived. Not heavy, but sticky. It was hard to distinguish individual snowflakes in the powder. School was out, so I didn't have to be anywhere the next day. My father was sound asleep on the kang, legs stretched beneath the table. The house stank of liquor from the plastic jug beside him. The sky turned completely dark. I opened the jug, poured some into my father's glass, and took a small mouthful. It was unbelievably sharp, and my brain felt like it was swelling, but I did get warmer. My father sat up.

—I dreamed that someone stole my liquor.

—It tastes disgusting.

He shifted his legs to make room for me. —Slow down, let it sit on your tongue and heat up before swallowing.

The next mouthful was even worse than the first, like a punch to the gut. My dad took shelled peanuts from a pocket and popped them into my mouth. He cleared his throat.

—Do you know the shape of Yanfen Street?

—It's a spiral.

—Correct. If you look from above it's like a mosquito coil, one circle after another.

He dipped a finger in the booze and drew on the table. —Here's where we live, on the east side. Your school is to the south, and my factory is north by Shadow Lake. It's closed down now.

—I heard they're still making tractors. Yang Saner got asked to go back.

—Oh, I guess the foreman's carrying on by himself. He won't need an engineer. So take your usual route to school but keep going, past Sun Yuxin's clinic, past Shadow Lake, past Coal-Fired Plant Number Four and across the train tracks, and you'll be at West Yanfen Street. You'll see a small church, and that's where your Youngest Aunt is. Her name is Zhang Yafeng.

—How do you know she's there?

—I went there once; it took me almost the whole day to walk there. Why don't you stay with your Youngest Aunt this winter? You can come home in the spring.

—I'm not going—I don't know her.

—She knows you. She came to visit right after you were born, so you've met. Bring the letter from Eldest Aunt, to prove you're my son.

—I'm not going.

—I've found a job in Xinmin, room and board provided, but I can't bring you.

—Are you going to be an engineer again?

—Night watchman. I'll be back at the start of spring. We'll both set off tomorrow morning, as soon as the snow stops. Now get some sleep.

It was almost noon when I woke up. My mouth still tasted of booze, and my head was heavy. My father was gone. I was lying under a blanket, with his army greatcoat folded by my side, beneath my woolen hat and gloves. A couple of red bean buns were on the table, wrapped in cloth. I sat up and looked out the window. The snow had stopped. A line of footprints cut through a field of dazzling white, heading toward the long-distance bus station. Across the road, the bike repair man was shoveling the snow from his front door, while his mute son Fatso kicked the drifts away. I ate the buns, rinsed the muslin cloth, and draped it across the stove. Then I dug out Eldest Aunt's letter and spread Liao Chenghu's map on the table. With my index figure, I traced the route my father would have taken. By my school, in words as tiny as housefly heads, it said: *Yanfen Elementary School, rebuilt in the 1950s on the site of Yanfen Township Schoolhouse.* Next to Coal-Fired Plant Number Four: *I don't know why it's called Number Four, I haven't heard of Numbers One through Three.* A long way to the west, almost on the map's edge, was a small building: *Bright Hall, mainly wood-built, two stories, 1920s; during the Cultural Revolution my struggle sessions took place here, and they stole two of my fingers.*

Although it said two stories, he'd made Bright Hall look so tall, you'd have thought it was ten. Beside his notes, he'd drawn a tiny figure with a square face and large eyes, apparently a girl.

I put the letter and map, plus all my holiday assignments, into my backpack, as well as a flashlight, in case I didn't arrive by sunset. Then I bundled up, locked the front door, and headed out. The snow reached up to my ankles. The dark clouds were gone, and sunlight was pouring down. The even coat of snow on all the low buildings gave them a rustic charm. There was a line at the public toilet—some people were carrying spittoons, while others cupped their ears for warmth, hand-rolled cigarettes drooping from their lips. The gates of my school were locked, and the elderly security guard was slowly clearing the snow with a broom. Old Dr. Sun stood outside his clinic doing his exercises, touching his toes with his fingertips. Through the window, I glimpsed his son, Sun Tianbo, asleep in one of the clinic's two massage chairs. After walking for a while, I saw Shadow Lake straight ahead of me, a pure white surface with no end in sight. I'd never come this far before. For the first time, I realized the vastness of Yanfen Street. As I turned onto a dirt track, old mining pits appeared on either side, along with little hillocks—a completely alien landscape. The sun hung low, and my legs were soaked. Up ahead, snow camouflaged the train tracks. I clambered up the one clear section. Two little girls, maybe three or four years younger than me, were building a snowman in the field ahead of me. I cleared my throat.

—How do I get to Bright Hall?

The taller girl glanced at me. —What?

—Bright Hall.

—Bride Hall? Aren't you too young to be getting married?

The other girl laughed. I probably looked a bit silly, all sweaty and laden down. Abruptly, she said:

—Train's coming.

—What?

—The train's coming, a green one.

I jumped off the tracks. A dark spot was speeding toward me, billowing steam. A dozen or more carriages, windows shut tight, reflecting the glare. I'd never seen a train up close before—it was unimaginably huge, roaring like a creature from another world. Clumps of snow fell off the poplar trees. I gaped for a moment, then reached into my backpack for the map. I wasn't mistaken: a little church should be up ahead. The tall girl was adding eyes to her snowman, one larger than the other, as if he were looking askance. The short girl approached. I pointed at the map and said:

—Look, it's down this road and around the corner, two stories, made of wood.

— Oh, you mean the Workers' Home.

The tall girl didn't bother looking away from her snowman. —Keep going, turn right, and it's at the top of the alleyway.

I put away my map. —Do you know Zhang Yafeng?

—She should be there now. Why are you looking for her?

— I have a letter for her.

I kept walking, and sure enough, behind a couple of withered trees, there was a two-story building marked "Workers' Home." I pushed open the wooden door and saw a narrow corridor, dark and clammy. To one side was a staircase and the mailroom, where some people were playing poker in a swirl of cigarette smoke. One of them pulled open the hatch.

—What?

—I'm looking for Zhang Yafeng.

—Second floor.

I walked up the stairs, past a portrait of a tall, golden-haired man cradling a lamb. Up above, a large room held a dozen rows of empty wooden benches facing a stage, on which two men and two women danced. A woman sat in the front row with a stereo in her lap, watching.

—Something wrong with your back, Old Gao?

—The music's too fast, I can't keep up.

—You were happy to fondle her palm all morning, but now that I want you to dance, you tell me the music's too fast?

Old Gao's partner interjected: —Fondle? More like a death grip.

—Go on, try again. If you can't do it, go home to your wife. Your body's broken and you still show up every day, tail between your legs.

The other man noticed me. —Who are you looking for?

—Is Zhang Yafeng here?

The seated woman turned.

—Here.

I walked toward her. She was wearing a dress and silk stockings, and had kicked off one of her shoes to rest her foot on the opposite knee.

—Who are you?

—I'm Zhang Guofu's son, Zhang Mo. Here's a letter my Eldest Aunt wrote to my dad.

She left the letter in its envelope. —Where's your father?

—He had to go to Xinmin for work. He sent me to you for the winter.

—Isn't he at the factory?

—It closed down. He's been out of work for two years now.

She straightened her skirt. Her face was square like my dad's, but her nose was higher. Same narrow eyes and pale skin, but with more creases, like clothes that had been folded too long.

—You brought money?

—No.

—That's bold of him, thinking he can use that letter as a banknote. What's in that backpack?

—Textbooks.

She kneaded her foot. —Do you still have that TV set?

—It's gone. How did you know we had one?

—I lugged two TVs back from the States—one for your grandpa, one for your father as a wedding present. Your Eldest Aunt almost killed me for not including her, but I'm not the Monkey God, maybe *he* could have managed three sets. So where did the TV go?

—We lent it to our neighbor.

She nodded. —Have you eaten?

—I had a big dinner last night.

—Old Gao, go tell the kitchen to make a bowl of hot noodle soup.

—Okay. I'll put it on my tab.

She pulled a couple of yuan from her stocking. —Take this.

The man disappeared down the stairs, and when the noodles arrived, they were topped with an egg. She rewound the tape and pressed Play, and the four people on the stage started dancing again.

After I had eaten, I knotted my sodden shoes, draped them over the heater, and sat next to Youngest Aunt with the great-coat over my feet. On the stage, the men and women kept

dancing, *clip-clop clip-clop*, a little more in unison now. Youngest Aunt yelled, Are you horses? Can't you turn your heads?
Night was falling, and the fluorescent lights came on. Eventually, the couples moved with the precision of drill troops.
Youngest Aunt lit a cigarette and smoked in silence. In the
warm room, I started to feel sleepy, but a growing cacoph-
ony kept me from drowsing off. I turned and saw that people
had filled the benches—four or five rows now, though the one
behind me had only one occupant: an old lady of maybe seventy. She stank a bit, and held a thin booklet close to her
eyes. The dancers took a break, sitting on the stage sipping tea.
When I turned around again, the short girl was walking down
the center aisle, a pair of mittens slung around her neck. She
was even tinier than I remembered. She went up to Youngest
Aunt.

—Ma, Pastor Lin is here.

Youngest Aunt turned to me: —Put on your shoes. Then
to the people on the stage: —You can go now; be in costume
by seven.

She stubbed out her cigarette, removed a booklet from her
purse, and settled onto the bench. The girl plopped down next
to her, pulling one foot up onto the seat, and leaned across to
me. —Another train came by after you left.

Youngest Aunt said: —This is your little cousin. Her real
name is Li Miao, but no one calls her that—she's our Gooseberry.

Gooseberry said to me: —Have you ever eaten a gooseberry?

—Yes, they're nothing but water.

—What grade are you in?

—Sixth.

—Have you learned binary quadratic equations?

All the benches were now packed, and a few people were standing at the back of the room. Old Gao emerged from backstage with a mike, plunked it on the side of the stage, and disappeared again.

A sudden hush washed over the room. The crisp sound of leather shoes. A tall, slender man in a dark suit came forward. He stepped up onto the stage, turned, and bowed deeply. A woman holding a bunch of scallions called out a greeting from the back of the room, and Youngest Aunt said, What's she squawking about? Sew her lips shut.

The man took the mike.

—The snow had stopped so I didn't cycle, yet I got here faster than if I were on my bike. Why do you think that is?

Someone shouted: —The Lord spirited you across the snow with a tailwind.

—I hitched a ride on Third Brother's goods cart.

Everyone burst out laughing, including Youngest Aunt.

—When I came before, the sky was clear and there was no sign of Third Brother—he was at the bus station picking up fancy young ladies. Yet today, I saw his empty cart speeding toward me. Why do you think that is?

Silence.

—The Almighty Lord sent him to bring me here.

The crowd applauded. Youngest Aunt sat on the edge of her seat with her hands folded in her lap.

—Let me ask you all, what kind of place is Yanfen Street? Someone called out: —It's a mud pit.

—Well said, and I guess that makes us mudskippers. How many of you know the history of this place?

—My dad told me there were mines when he moved here.

—How old is your dad now?

An elderly voice croaked: —Seventy-five, just keeping my belly full while I wait to die.

—Don't talk like that—Adam lived to be seven hundred and seventy-seven, you're a child compared to him. You're right, though, Yanfen Street did have mines, back in the sixties. This place has a complicated past. Before the Manchus breached the Great Wall, this was an army base that saw a lot of battle. In the late Qing dynasty, burglars and bandits flourished here. Then the Japanese arrived and would hack you to pieces for just walking down the street. In the early 1940s, a rumor of buried treasure circulated. The Nationalist government sent people to dig up the land, but they came up empty. During the Cultural Revolution, coal was found, and about two hundred miners were recruited from among the downtrodden—rural migrants, unregistered households, demoted rightists, injured laborers—and corralled in Yanfen Township. After Liberation, "township" sounded too old-fashioned, and the name was changed to Yanfen Street. Still the same people, though. If I had to guess, I'd say that quite a few of the present company have done things they shouldn't and been stuck in jail for a bit. I bet a few owe money and they're lying low here. And others are planning to get more booze after the service.

The man's suit and pale blue shirt had seen better days. He was maybe forty years old, with short hair neatly combed to the side and faint stubble. When he spoke, one hand gripped the base of the mike, while the other made small, precise gestures. His deep-set eyes were sharp, gleaming in their hollows.

—Like I said before, I'm a sinner, too.

He undid the last button on his jacket.

—I've hurt people. I broke someone's arm—did seven years in prison for that. But then what happened?

Someone in the crowd called out: —You found the Lord.

—The Lord sent me to prison so I could grow close to him, to see him, to lean on him. How many times have I read the Bible cover to cover?

The crowd: —Seven!

—I read it once a year and can finally see myself clearly. During my third year, someone stabbed me clean through the lung. It was the Bible that saved me—and when I lived, I prayed for the man who stabbed me. Just before I was released, the old man who taught me Scripture passed. He left me his Bible. I came out of Jiamusi Prison and headed for Harbin, where I knelt in Saint Sophia Cathedral. A pigeon landed on my shoulder and flew south. The Lord was telling me to bring the Good News southward. That's how I ended up here. When I recall that bird, I think of a hymn praising the Lord. I've already taught it to you all. Please take your neighbor's hand.

> Mountains can move, hills can shift,
> But the Lord's love will never drift
> He staves off sin, far as east from west
> His kindness raises me above the rest
> He will keep alive the flickering light,
> And tend to the sparrow soaring in flight

Most people were on their feet now, swaying and singing. Youngest Aunt held both Gooseberry's hand and mine and joined in softly. Then the man opened a thick book with a

black leather cover and grimy pages and led the congregation in reading from their little mimeographed booklets for
a long time. His next prayer also dragged on, and when they
were finally done, he made his way through the crowd with
a cardboard box. Youngest Aunt put in five yuan—half my
month's allowance. When he reached me, I said, I don't have
any money.

—That's okay, it's enough that you're here.

He knelt in front of Gooseberry. —And what have you got
for me today?

She reached into her pocket and pulled out a stone. —This
was one of my snowman's eyes.

—What about your snowman?

—He's sleeping, so he doesn't need to see right now.

The old lady behind me said: —Young man, my foot's rot-
ting, I can barely stand—I always feel better after hearing you
speak. Just make me well again.

—You're mixing up body and soul—go to a doctor.

—My grandson's parents don't care about him. Please pray
for him.

The pastor nodded.

The old woman put half a yuan into the box. —Let me
touch your book.

He did so and then moved on to the next person. When
he was finished, he unhurriedly pulled on his outdoor clothes
and said, Now please enjoy the performance.

He tipped his hat. —Thank you, Ms. Zhang.

Youngest Aunt nodded, and he walked out.

A third of the congregation left, and the four people on
the stage started dancing energetically. Several onlookers
stood and clapped to the beat, and someone whistled. The

two women's skirts revealed flashes of thigh with each swirl, and Old Gao's forehead glistened with sweat. A few times, his hand slid down his partner's waist. Youngest Aunt watched silently. Two people at the back of the room began quarreling, but they were quickly drowned out by applause. A drunk person got punched in the face and staggered away clutching his head. By the time the whole thing was over, I was so sleepy I could barely keep my eyes open. Through my drooping eyelids, I saw Youngest Aunt flatten a beer can with a stomp.

A dream threaded through my night, unfolding in fits and starts. My dad and Liao Chenghu were fishing on the shore of Shadow Lake. I walked through a drizzle toward them. They turned to look at me, and I saw that they were both teenagers. I said, You knew each other when you were young? My father said, What do you mean? We've just met. Liao Chenghu said, Watch, I'm going to catch a big one. I sat between them, impaling worms onto their hooks. A fish leaped from the surface of the lake, its tail scattering water droplets. My father turned to me and said, My name is Zhang Guofu, and I want to be an engineer when I grow up. What's your name? I said nothing. His face was smooth and youthful, the collar of his green army jacket was open, and water dripped from his inky bangs. Liao Chenghu said, So listen, I've talked it over with Guofu, I'm a clay sculptor, and he's going to make me a pedestal—what are you going to do? I said, You have a bite. Liao Chenghu gripped his rod with both hands as it bent violently—he still had all ten fingers. My father stood to help him reel the fish in, and I wrapped my arms around his waist. Effortlessly, the fish dragged us into the water. The other two shrugged off their clothes and started swimming. Ahead, the fish arched its body and headed into the depths. It was strange-looking, unusually fat and crusted with mud. The two teenagers dove after it, but I was afraid—I didn't know where it was going. My head rose above the water. The raindrops were fatter now, drumming down on my face. Thunder rumbled. As the current dragged me away, I opened my mouth to call the other two back, but water surged into me.

I opened my eyes. Sun was hitting my face. Ever since I was little, I'd known that the fish in Shadow Lake couldn't be eaten and that no one ever went fishing there—but I didn't know why. What inspired this dream? I was in a double bed, and Gooseberry was sitting on the edge, combing her hair. I sat up and rubbed my eyes. The window framed a vacant patch of land on which snow had been swept into little mounds. A man with a metal bucket was squatting on the ground, carving something on a wooden board.

Gooseberry said: —You didn't answer me yesterday. Have you learned binary quadratic equations?

I felt like my body was still floating. —Not yet. We're doing them next semester.

The room had a large wardrobe and a dressing table, and two red leather suitcases shoved in a corner, covered with a pink cloth. My shoes hung upside down from a heater near the bed. I realized from the sloping ceiling that we were in an attic.

—Ma says you're family. Where do you come from?

—My father is your mother's older brother; I come from the same place you do.

—How long are you staying?

—For the winter. I can work to earn my keep.

—After you went to sleep last night, Ma and I had to clean the lecture hall on our own.

—Sorry, I just got here. What grade are you in?

—Third.

—Which school?

—Yanfen Elementary.

—Me too. How come I've never seen you? What's your form teacher's name?

—Mr. Jin.

—Voice like a broken gong? Funny walk?

—Exactly. Who's yours?

—You wouldn't know him—they all change in grade five. Where's your father? I should say hello.

She flicked her plait forward. —Put on your shoes, we're going to fetch some coal.

—I haven't eaten.

—We don't have breakfast in this house. Oh, and you kicked me all night. I told my mother. You'll sleep in the hall tonight.

Downstairs, Youngest Aunt had a basin of hot water at her feet. She dipped a cloth and began wiping the doorframe. When she saw us, she pointed toward the yard.

—Do you know those words?

Gooseberry and I walked toward the man carving the wooden board. Quite a bit of sawdust had piled up. Gooseberry squinted.

—Bright Hall.

—You can read that?

—Ma taught me.

The man blew the sawdust off the board and began painting it red. Youngest Aunt said:

—Have you got the basket?

Gooseberry ran back inside to fetch a bamboo basket.

—Lunch at noon, dance practice later.

—I know, Ma.

I'd assumed we would be heading to Coal-Fired Plant Number Four, but instead Gooseberry led me in the other direction, past some low buildings. We walked through several alleyways and passed a woman in a leather coat sitting on her doorstep, peeling garlic, with a spotted dog slumped by her side.

—Where are you off to, Gooseberry?

—Just for a walk.

Our destination turned out to be a tofu factory with a partially frozen stream of filthy water and debris trickling from its doorway. A line of people were waiting for fresh tofu. Thick fog coated the back of the building, where there was a pile of yellow briquettes with dark splotches. Gooseberry said, We want all the ones with black in them. I started grabbing. Some were still hot and scorched my hands. After a while, the back door opened and a middle-aged woman in sleeve protectors and boots came out with a basket of coal to dump on the heap.

—I was so busy this week, I didn't make it to the service.

—Pastor Lin told us it doesn't matter if we can't go, as long as our hearts are present.

I glanced at Gooseberry. She must have said this many times, the words fell so easily from her lips.

—Who's this?

—My cousin. He's visiting.

The woman went back inside, and we finished filling our basket. I wasn't good at picking—some coals looked fine to me but crumbled at my touch. The woman came out again with a bag of tofu scraps and a bag of briquettes that, though broken, were black and unused. Gooseberry thanked her. On our way back, I carried the coal, so Gooseberry only had to manage the tofu. She skipped along, pirouetting.

—Don't drop the tofu.

—My pa's a dancer.

—Mine's an engineer.

—My parents performed in America, back before I was born.

I said nothing.

She twirled again. —Ma came back but Pa didn't. He stayed there to have fun.

The new signboard was ready by the time we got back. One side read "Workers' Home" in black on a white background, and the other side read "Bright Hall" in red. We delivered the coal and tofu to the kitchen, then sat down for lunch. Afterward, Gooseberry went off for dance practice with Youngest Aunt, and I tagged along. As I watched, I thought she deserved to be named after a more graceful bird than the goose. Now she extended one leg over her head, now she stretched it to the side. When she stumbled a little, Youngest Aunt rapped her on the ankle with her stick.

—Open up. Again!

And so Gooseberry repeated the exercise. I got out an assignment and sat writing on my lap. After a while, Youngest Aunt turned to me.

—Zhang Mo, are you strong?

Gooseberry said: —He carried the basket back with one hand.

—Am I interrupting your homework?

—No, I'm done.

—Come here and lift Gooseberry.

I walked up onto the stage.

—Take her by the waist and raise her over your head.

I lifted her and she soared, scarcely heavier than the coal.

—Hold her there.

Youngest Aunt adjusted Gooseberry's legs with the stick.

By the end of the session, I was drenched in sweat. Gooseberry had been hit quite a few times, and so had I, but while Youngest Aunt tapped me, she beat Gooseberry for real. That night, I wrapped myself in blankets and slept on the stage. The bed wasn't big enough, anyway. The floor was hard, but there was space to toss and turn.

In the morning, we went out to sell beer bottles and scrap paper. While studying Liao Chenghu's map, I'd noticed a banyan tree to the north of Bright Hall, the only plant he'd marked amid all the buildings: *Banyan, a southern tree that somehow ended up here. About twenty-five meters tall, broader than three arm spans. In the summer, its shadow is six or seven meters across, enough to nap under. Generations of people pass, but it remains standing.* Gooseberry didn't remember seeing such a tree, and she bet me it wasn't there. We went looking for it, and sure enough, it was gone—cut down who knows how many years ago, leaving just a thick stump, mottled with snow, exactly where the map said it would be. As we wandered back, a neighbor gave us a little pork and pickled vegetables to take home.

On Saturday night, lying alone on the stage, I thought about the afternoon's rehearsal. Youngest Aunt had beat Gooseberry when I dropped her, insisting that her weight hadn't been centered correctly. Still, I hoped Youngest Aunt would go on teaching us both—my legs were strong, and I would make a good partner for Gooseberry. I stood up and kicked high in the darkness. Gooseberry could get her leg all the way up to her ear, probably because she was so short.

I wondered how my father was doing in his new job. I ought to have asked for his address so I could write. Youngest Aunt wasn't like my mother, who'd never hit me, but whose thoughts remained mysterious. Youngest Aunt was easy to read: the solemnity with which she pronounced Pastor Lin's name, her giddiness as she awaited his arrival. Some people said no one knew where Pastor Lin lived, and some claimed that he changed residences daily. Others said he'd been called by God and would soon be heading south. Youngest Aunt muttered, What's there to fear, you can go anywhere if you have true faith.

Youngest Aunt woke up very early each morning and read her little booklet. Gooseberry and I weren't allowed to hang around while she did this. Next, she swept the courtyard, then started the singing and dancing lessons. Her voice was melodious, but I'd never seen her really dance—she taught by talking. She walked very fast and didn't eat much. It occurred to me that she still hadn't returned Eldest Aunt's letter—I wondered if she'd read it. The letter said, *Guofu, she's your little sister after all, and now she's moved to Yanfen Street, you ought to go see her. She won't listen to us, and talks always end in a fight about the past. We can't decide her fate, nor her child's. The girl is hers—she insisted on having her, and refused to denounce the father Big Liu as a spy when he fled the country. She lost her job because of that. All of this is her life, her business. We remember the good things about her. Ever since she was a kid, she wanted to be the best at everything. And when she falls for someone, she doesn't hold back, she gives herself completely to him, even if she ends up getting hurt. Haven't you realized that yet? We followed the crowd, but she forged her own path, and it's hard to say whose way worked out better. Don't you think so?* My father had gotten me to read him this letter, so I remembered it very well. We never replied.

I heard footsteps on the stairs and quickly burrowed back under the sheets, eyes fixed on the doorway. No one came in. Something moved on the stairs, and after a while I heard footsteps again. It was Gooseberry, in woolen pajamas, hugging her bedding. She dumped it five or six meters from me and tucked herself in. I went over—her eyes were shut. I handed her my hot water bottle.

—Did Youngest Aunt hit you?

She was silent.

—Are you crying?

—No. Go to sleep.

—We agreed the stage would be my spot. What are you doing here?

—I'll tell Ma to kick you out tomorrow, then I'll sleep here all by myself.

More movement on the stairs. Someone was murmuring out there.

—Forget about sleeping, I'm wide awake. I could turn a somersault.

—Yeah, right. Your legs are stiff, like logs—you can't even do the splits.

—Tell me why you're crying, or my hands might slip when I'm holding you, and you'll land on your head.

She sat up abruptly and looked straight at me.

—Pastor Lin once told us there was a man named Jonah, he lived in a whale's stomach for three days and nights, but he didn't die, he just floated across the ocean. Do you think I could do that?

—Why not? There's a lot of space in a whale's stomach—it's probably more comfortable than a ship.

—Old Gao is here.

—What?

—He comes twice a week, he's in charge of the Workers' Home.

—Does it belong to his family?

—I don't know. Anyway, what he says goes.

—Didn't they hang a sign up a couple of days ago? It's Bright Hall now.

—With his permission. Pastor Lin only arrived three months ago, and we've been here half a year—but Old Gao's had forty years here. My mother says he worships Pastor Lin too, but his attitude changes very quickly. When he likes you everything's fine, but when he doesn't, he gives you a hard time. He kicked us out last fall, though he let us back again. Ma's never been scared of him. Whenever he comes to the attic, she chases him away. She said we've suffered all kinds of hardships, there's nothing to fear, at worst we'll go live under a bridge.

—Why is Youngest Aunt raising you alone?

—Isn't it obvious? There's only the two of us.

—Why doesn't she ever dance? Sometimes she strikes a pose, and it's beautiful.

—She swore that she would never dance with anyone except my father. Go to sleep.

—I don't want to sleep, I want to practice lifts.

—You're weird, practicing lifts in the middle of the night.

—I can do a grand jeté too, and I can get farther than you.

I did a couple of jumps, and Gooseberry laughed.

—You move like a duck.

I leaped over to the lectern and noticed that one of its side panels was moldy. When I nudged it with my foot, it crumbled.

—Hey, there's something in here.

Gooseberry crawled over to look.

—You have thin arms. See if you can fish it out.

Gooseberry rested her chin on the lectern and stuck her arm in. There it was, a parcel in several sheets of white paper. We unwrapped a little figurine: a girl, naked, standing on one leg with the other stretching back.

Gooseberry stared at it. —Is this clay?

—I think so.

—Why isn't she wearing anything?

—Maybe the sculptor ran out of time.

—Look, her ears are different sizes.

I examined the figurine. Sure enough, one ear was normal, with detailed whorls, the other somewhat smaller and shrunken, like a clump of unrisen dough. I held the little statue in my palm and stared at it for a while. It was heavy, and there was something tentative about the girl's smile. Gooseberry snatched it and returned to her bedding.

—What are you doing? I saw it first.

—So what? I pulled it out.

—But you couldn't have done that without me.

—This is Bright Hall, where my family lives, so of course it belongs to me. Can't you tell she's meant to be dancing? That means she belongs to me twice over.

All of a sudden, I remembered that Liao Chenghu's map had a human figure next to Bright Hall.

—This has to mean something.

—Stop talking or Ma will come down.

She slid beneath the covers and pulled the blanket over her head. I shoved her a few times, but she didn't react.

—Make sure you don't fart, you'll suffocate in there.

She didn't stir, so I had no choice but to wriggle back beneath my own blankets.

The next evening, a blizzard unleashed what seemed like a whole winter's worth of snow at once. Despite the weather, the congregation for Pastor Lin's sermon was even bigger than the previous week. People stood in the outer passageway and squashed in next to us, their clothes dappled with snowflakes. Youngest Aunt took Gooseberry on her lap. She was wearing an old silk scarf and had applied a little makeup but hadn't managed to hide the dark circles below her eyes. The old woman who'd sat behind me last time didn't seem to be there. Pastor Lin told us two stories: Cain killing his brother, and Abraham sacrificing his son. *Jehovah said unto Cain, Why art thou wroth? and why is thy countenance fallen? If thou doest well, shall it not be lifted up? and if thou doest not well, sin coucheth at the door; and unto thee shall be its desire; but do thou rule over it. And Cain told Abel his brother. And it came to pass, when they were in the field, that Cain rose up against Abel his brother, and slew him. And Jehovah said unto Cain, What hast thou done?* Maybe because she hadn't slept well the night before, Gooseberry was running a fever. She was still warm now, drowsing in Youngest Aunt's arms. When he was done with Cain, Pastor Lin moved on to Abraham. Someone in the congregation asked:

—Pastor Lin, do you have any children?

The pastor didn't answer, but went on talking about Abraham piling kindling onto his altar, tying up his son, and holding up the sharp knife, ready to plunge.

—Pastor Lin, if you had a child, would you bring him up the mountain?

The pastor looked at the questioner.

—I don't know; the Lord has not extinguished all my

doubts yet. He is leading my steps. There is a passage in the Epistle to the Hebrews that I offer to you, my friend: *It is a fearful thing to fall into the hands of the living God.* Yet this is really good fortune, and ultimately leads us to eternal happiness. When the Lord teaches us, we must listen; when he speaks Scripture before us, we must receive it; when he summons us, we must answer, Here I am.

After we'd prayed, Pastor Lin came around with his box. I noticed Youngest Aunt shaking a little as she put half a yuan in. —Zhang Mo, take Gooseberry upstairs, I need to talk to the pastor.

Pastor Lin said: —No need for that, just speak—we're family.

Youngest Aunt hugged Gooseberry.

—I've spent so much time listening to you, and I want to ask, if I sincerely believe in the Lord, will the Lord hear my wishes?

—He hears you, but he may not grant them, because he has a greater wish that enfolds you within it. Your wish is a drop of water, and the Lord's is an ocean.

—If the Lord has been refining me in his crucible all my life, and I still see no hope, then how can I believe? Where is the Lord?

—Do you have something you can depend on?

Youngest Aunt thought about it. —Yes.

—Everything we rely on, we call the Lord. Do you have a conscience?

—Yes.

—Your conscience is the voice of the Lord.

He brushed his hand across Gooseberry's forehead. —Gooseberry has a fever.

—I think she caught a cold last night.

Pastor Lin fished a few tablets from his pocket. —I always carry these with me. Give her half a pill at a time.

Youngest Aunt took them. —We were talking about wishes. Do you know what I wish for, Pastor?

Pastor Lin paused a moment. —I have an idea.

—Do you know what I depend on?

—I have an idea.

—There was something you said in your sermon that I'd also like to say to you.

—What was that?

—When you summon me, I must answer: here I am. The south isn't that far away, I have no home, and I have two legs; I can walk south.

Pastor Lin looked at Youngest Aunt. His eyes turned golden.

—I see.

Then he moved on to the next person.

After the service, Youngest Aunt and I cleaned up the lecture hall. Gooseberry had taken her medicine and gone to bed. Youngest Aunt hummed as she circled the room twice with the broom, then fetched hot water to wipe the windows. I tried to help, but she said, Take a break, watch your auntie work. I sat on a pew as she went up the ladder to get at the highest panes. I'd never seen her so happy.

—I read your Eldest Aunt's letter. In old age, she's become at least half-wise. Your father once slapped me across the face, blaming me for the black mark on his record because of what happened with Gooseberry's father. I didn't hit him back, but I turned around and never went home again. I'd gotten to that age without anyone hitting me. When your Eldest Aunt and dad were kids, they never said a word; I was the only one who spoke up. One time, someone beat your dad up, and he said to the guy, Just you wait, I'll go fetch my little sister. What a loser—make sure you don't end up like him.

I nodded.

—In '68, when the Red Guards converged on Beijing for the Great Networking, I was the only one from our family who took part. We ate for free wherever we went, and everyone sang together on the train, whether we knew each other or not. When I lost my shoe in the crowd, I looked around and saw someone else's shoe on the ground, so I just put that on. Your Eldest Aunt and your father tried to stop me, but when I got home, they pestered me, asking if I'd seen Chairman Mao. Though I hadn't, I said yes, his face glowed red and he was over seven feet tall. They actually believed me, and wished they'd gone, too.

—Where else have you been?

—I wasn't there when your grandpa and grandma died, and now that I think about it, I ought to have been; maybe they had some last words for me. The way your grandma used to cook rice porridge, it tasted sweet even though she never added sugar—I still don't know how she did it.

She was quiet for a while, concentrating on the window she was cleaning. The room was silent, aside from her even breathing. As her body stretched atop the ladder, her hair almost brushed the ceiling, just like Gooseberry's when I lifted her. She was dancing, but I didn't know with whom. From downstairs came the sound of a bicycle stopping. Youngest Aunt dismounted, dropped the rag into the water basin, and stood watching the door, with one hand on her chest and the other clutching her skirt. It wasn't Pastor Lin but Old Gao. As usual, his forehead was shiny. He stood in the doorway.

—Yafeng, could you come here for a moment?

She turned and bent to pick up the rag. —I'm busy.

—Come here, please, there's something I need to tell you.

Youngest Aunt stayed where she was, swirling the cloth around in the water.

—Someone stabbed Pastor Lin.

She stood and turned back to face him.

—In the alleyway, about two hundred meters from here.

She wrung the cloth dry and wiped her hands. —Is he dead?

—Yes.

She followed him out without even looking at me. I ran to the attic, scooped up Gooseberry in the greatcoat, and grabbed my backpack. Downstairs a small crowd huddled in the alleyway. Pastor Lin was facedown, legs ramrod straight, his wide-brimmed hat a short distance away. A puddle of blood oozed from him, glistening by the light of the streetlamp. I saw his intestines slithering out into the grime, and noticed a tattoo on the back of his neck: a pair of wings. Snow thrashed through the air, spattering the pastor's body. Youngest Aunt and Old Gao stood near him.

One of the bystanders said: —Someone's gone to the police station.

Youngest Aunt swatted at the air. —Did anyone see who did it?

No one answered. She knelt and rifled through Pastor Lin's coat pockets. In the left one, she found his Bible, spotless, and in the right, a pink silk spring scarf, brand-new, with the label still attached, stained with blood. Youngest Aunt clamped the Bible under her arm, shook out the scarf to examine it, then rolled Pastor Lin over. Large patches of blood covered his chest and belly. His mouth gaped open, though his eyes were shut. Death had aged him in an instant. Youngest Aunt stripped off his jacket and laid it over him. Someone shouted, The attic! I turned to look. The blizzard had dumped so much snow on Bright Hall, the wooden supports holding up the attic had collapsed under its weight. Old Gao said, Fuck, where did all this snow come from? He started pelting back to the hall, but turned after a few paces, took off his coat, draped it over Youngest Aunt's shoulders, and then headed for the hall again. Several of the others followed him.

Youngest Aunt stood there for a while. Then she walked over to the streetlamp and flipped through the Bible by its light, pacing back and forth. She raised one hand in a gesture. I heard her murmur, Here am I, Abraham replied. Then she stuck the Bible into the pocket of Old Gao's coat. Finally, she seemed to notice I was there. Feeling in Old Gao's pockets, she found twenty yuan.

—Take Gooseberry to your home, maybe your dad will be there by now.

—He won't be.

—Bring her there and wait for him. Tell her I had some business to take care of, and I'll catch up with the two of you.

—You can't go—my legs are too stiff for me to be Gooseberry's partner.

—I'll come and find you. Tell your dad to keep track of everything Gooseberry eats or drinks; I don't want to owe him anything.

—Where are you going?

She patted her pocket but said nothing. Then she ripped the label off the scarf, wrapped it around her neck, and started walking south, past the piles of lumber. I didn't know her destination; maybe it was the same as the green train's. She didn't look back. The blood-spotted scarf danced through the air. The streetlamp cast its light over her. Then she was gone.

I pulled the map out of my backpack and started walking toward home, carrying Gooseberry on my back. After passing by Coal-Fired Plant Number Four, I got a bit lost. At night, the landscape was unfamiliar again. I studied the map and picked a direction. Gooseberry's cheek rested against my neck, scalding hot. I grabbed a handful of snow and rubbed it across her face. After a long while, I saw the gate of the plant and realized we'd gone in a circle. I chose another path and kept walking. A tall figure appeared in the darkness. My whole body went limp. I said:

—I don't know who you are; I just want to get home.

He didn't answer. I walked over to find Gooseberry's snowman, one eye missing, the other gazing indifferently.

Gooseberry stirred.

—Cousin, is America on this map of yours?

—Yes, it's not far from here.

She shut her eyes and went back to sleep. I took a breath and struggled through the darkness, murmuring a prayer for my father's return.

2

On the rooftops, the snow was pure white and flaky, while the stuff on the road had been stamped into ice and mud. The

north wind howled. Down the street came Liu Ding with a
heavy box of tea eggs for his grandmother. They were piping
hot, so he wasn't cold. Liu Ding once asked his grandmother
why he had such a weird name. Kids his age had proper names
like Yang Xu or Sun Tianbo. Even Fatso's real name was Dong
Jiayuan.

—What's wrong with your name?

—Nothing, it just feels a bit—you know. My teacher said
it's great, but it doesn't sound like a real name. She wanted to
know how I got it.

Grandma turned to look in the direction of Yanfen Middle
School.

—Don't waste your energy worrying about that. Just make
sure you study hard, so you can offer me good food to eat
when I'm dead.

—Did my mother choose my name?

—No, she just left a note saying she was going to Beijing,
asking me to look after her child, claiming she'd be back very
soon. Her conscience must have been eaten by dogs.

—And the note?

—I threw it away.

—I took your surname, but where did the "Ding" come
from?

When they were almost home, Grandma pointed. —Your
mother abandoned you at that intersection, which is shaped
like the character "ding," 丁.

And so in the winter of 1993, at age thirteen, Liu Ding
first learned the origin of his name. But when he thought
about it, he decided there was no need to tell his teacher—he
had to repeat the grade, so he would soon have a different
teacher anyway.

Liu Ding was large for his age, about five foot seven and 130 pounds. He'd gotten into a fight at school the day before and had beaten a couple of older boys to a pulp, leaving one with broken bones and the other with a concussion. The principal wanted to send him to reform school, because this wasn't the first time he'd lashed out over a small thing—in fact, he couldn't remember afterward how the fight got started. Grandma showed up at the school with a gift of tea eggs, and when that failed, she flung herself onto the concrete floor of the principal's office in front of the other kids' parents and started writhing around, insisting that she was a pensioner—sending Liu Ding away would be tantamount to killing her, as she had nothing else to live for. Why not just give her a rope to hang herself with right here? The other parents stared at the crazed movements of this tiny old woman, in her grease-spattered trousers and dilapidated cotton shoes. The school finally agreed—as long as Liu Ding was kept back a year. While all his classmates advanced to a classroom on the second level, he'd stay on the ground floor. The principal wrote it all up, and the parents pressed their fingerprints onto the paper. The principal asked Grandma:

—What do you normally give Liu Ding to eat?

—Not much. Sometimes we only have one meal a day.

—Then how did he get to be so tall?

—Maybe it's from his dad; maybe his father is tall, too.

Liu Ding's grandmother was a little disturbed—or maybe not disturbed, but she got agitated easily. She had suffered two serious blows in her life. The first was when her husband was killed in a mining accident, along with another twenty-odd people. The tragedy's scale made it easier to bear—every family had lost someone, but still. The second was when Liu

Ding's mother disappeared without a trace, washing her hands of him. Compared to these losses, Grandma felt that her husband's being denounced as a counterrevolutionary rightist and banished to Yanfen Street wasn't that big of a deal. At least no one died that time. And when he was posthumously rehabilitated with the changing times, she managed to get a bit of compensation and a house, which she would never leave— Grandpa's grave was behind the former mine, and she couldn't abandon it.

Back home, Liu Ding remained quiet. Grandma clicked her tongue.

—Well, I hope you're pleased with yourself.

—Grandma, I told you you're touched in the head—now do you believe me?

Grandma took the tea egg box from him and put it on the kang.

—I was faking, couldn't you tell? I did it for you.

Pretending to be mad is its own kind of madness, Liu Ding thought. He felt his spirits sink. Pretty soon, everyone would have heard about what happened in the principal's office. It was already awkward that Grandma hawked eggs near his school. She cooked them first thing every morning. Once people knew she was crazy, his life would be over. He wished he could go back and start another fight, a bigger one that would leave everyone dead.

Liu Ding was talented at fighting, with quick reflexes and a knack for choosing exactly the right angle of attack. Against a shorter opponent, he would grab the other guy's hair and bring his knee up to smash his face. With someone taller, a kick to the groin and a fist to the chin usually sufficed. He was tenacious: even when pinned down, he'd never yield, but always found a way to hit back; if he managed to get back on top, he'd show no mercy, refusing to stop till his opponent's face was destroyed. He only fought with people his own age, though, and didn't pick on elementary schoolers, the way some middle schoolers did. He'd been a victim himself, one summer during elementary school. Though he put up a fierce fight, a bunch of bigger kids pinned him to the ground and took not just his lunch—rice with tomato-egg stir-fry, which Grandma had gotten up early to make—but also his trousers. How mortifying, having to retrieve his schoolbag bare-assed, blood streaming from his nose. He couldn't make it stop, and in the end he got so frustrated he punched himself a couple of times. Every time he recalled this utter humiliation, he thought of Grandma tottering on her bound feet outside the school gates, clutching her wooden box in the hot sun and calling out to customers. The next day, he filled a sack with sand, hung it from a tree in their yard, and started pummeling. From then on, he repeated this routine for an hour every day. Even if there had been rain and the sand was hard as iron, he persisted till his hands were swollen. Now he could have taken on the boys who'd attacked him, but he never saw them again.

Liu Ding opened the box and ate a couple of tea eggs. Quite salty. It was just past the winter solstice, and paper decorations adorned the windows. The punching bag dangled from the tree branch like a giant cocoon. His classes didn't matter now, because next week they would start over. Liu Ding's grades were pretty good, particularly in languages and history—his memory was strong—though he struggled with math and physics. Teachers preferred straightforward students: strong or weak, studious or disruptive. Though Liu Ding was in between, most teachers pigeonholed him anyway: he was bad. Only Old Zhao, the security guard, didn't seem to need to think in categories.

Old Zhao had a bit of a hump from a rounded spine, but he could stand up straight when he wanted to, gaining a few inches. The kids called him "sir," because he was also the ethics teacher and disciplined students. Given the circumstances, an ethics teacher was rather crucial: only one in ten students made it from junior to senior high, while the rest left the area for vocational schools or simply abandoned education altogether and spent their days roaming Yanfen Street. These boys and girls often hung out at Spring Breeze Dance Hall and Red Star Billiard Room, heads lolling, constantly smoking, still not starved to death. Before Old Zhao, their ethics teacher had been Teacher Gao, a bully who eventually left to manage some sort of "Workers' Home" in the north. Sounded like a promotion. The first day Old Zhao showed up, he was in a white shirt and blue canvas trousers with the legs rolled up, a hand towel around his neck. At the lunch break, a senior stood smoking in the doorway, while the girl by his side, out of uniform, perched on the back of her bicycle, eating melon seeds. Old Zhao walked over.

—Put that out.

The boy looked him up and down. —Who are you?

—Put it out.

—Why don't you do your job and stoke the boiler?

Old Zhao's leg shot out, sweeping the boy to the ground. Then he produced a pair of handcuffs and locked him to the fence. The girl ran away, scattering melon seeds as she fled.

After this incident, all the students knew who he was. Have you heard? The new security guard, he has his own handcuffs. Ruthless. Liu Ding heard the story, too—it amused him. Old Zhao lived in the gatehouse, which wasn't heated, so the school had given him a little stove where he could boil water and cook his meals. When you came to school on a winter morning, you'd see smoke snaking from the chimney. Old Zhao would be squatting by the gate, brushing his teeth in long johns and plastic flip-flops, big toes curled over. The water froze as soon as he spat it out. Liu Ding thought he must have been a soldier—he'd never seen anyone using such vigor, thrusting the toothbrush into his mouth like a harpoon. This made him feel close to Old Zhao, because Liu Ding also dreamed of joining the army.

Liu Ding wanted to make his way in the world as soon as he finished junior high. He believed he had what it took to be a soldier: strength and no fear of suffering. If he succeeded, he'd surely make a name for himself. If he failed, he could go to Beijing, because Grandma had told him that when his mother left, she'd said she was headed to the capital. Before that, she had worked the cash register at Spring Breeze Dance Hall, and had sometimes even danced. He'd heard that she was a taxi dancer, five yuan for three dances, but no photographs of her remained, and Grandma refused to say any more. He'd once stationed himself at the dance hall and confronted a bunch of people; they said his mother was about five foot five, long-haired and square-faced, with a bit of an underbite, a pigeon-toed walk, and a slender waist. She smoked Red Plum Blossom cigarettes. The most distinctive thing about her was that one of her ears was noticeably smaller than the other, though she kept them hidden beneath her hair. Maybe he could find her in some Beijing dance hall.

On one occasion, his class was trying to get a broom from the classroom cupboard, but the lock was rusted shut. No matter how they jiggled the key, it wouldn't budge. The teacher told Liu Ding to try, but he only succeeded in snapping the key off in the lock. The latch was too sturdy to break. He dragged the cupboard away from the wall, but the teacher said:

—Stop it—at this rate you'll be bringing it home with you. Go get Old Zhao.

Liu Ding knocked on the gatehouse door. —Sir?

—It's not locked.

Liu Ding went in and found Old Zhao sitting on the bed, wiping a harmonica with a cloth. He played the harmonica? Why hadn't Liu Ding seen him playing before?

—Sir, our teacher needs you.

Old Zhao put the harmonica on his pillow.

—Just call me Old Zhao.

Standing before the cupboard, Old Zhao studied it. —If I force it open, it might break.

—That's fine.

Old Zhao grabbed the side of the cupboard and wrenched the entire door off, lock and all.

Liu Ding went back to the gatehouse after school and knocked, and again Old Zhao said:

—It's not locked.

Liu Ding went in.

—Sir, my name is Liu Ding. I live at the west end of Yanfen Street.

—Did another cupboard get stuck?

—No, I want to arm wrestle with you.

It was an autumn evening, and the daylight was beginning to slip away, though Old Zhao's lights were still off. An acrid aroma wafted from the fragments of burning coal. The kettle boiled, and Old Zhao lifted it off the stove.

—How old are you?

—Thirteen.

—I have to sweep the field; it's covered in leaves.

—And when you're done?

—Then I'll burn the leaves and make my rounds.

—You think I can't beat you?

—No, I don't arm wrestle.

With that, he grabbed a large broom from a corner of the room and walked out. Liu Ding followed behind. There was no one on the field, just a layer of leaves from the poplar trees that surrounded it, their branches now almost bare. Some of their bark had split, revealing yellow flesh. Old Zhao slowly swept the leaves into heaps.

A teacher walked by, wheeling a bicycle.

—You've got your work cut out, Mr. Zhao?

—That I do.

—So many leaves, and there'll be more tomorrow.

—I'll be glad when they're all gone.

The teacher cycled off. Old Zhao swept for about an hour, then got out his matches and set the heap of leaves alight. There was just a small ring of flames at the top of the pile, but they spewed smoke, and each time the wind blew, it rose as if signaling to someone in the distance.

—Sir, were you ever a soldier?

Still holding the broom, Old Zhao stared at the fire heap.

—No.

—Please tell me—I want to be a soldier, too.

—I was never a soldier, I'm just a regular person.

—Where are you from?

—Why do you want to be a soldier? Can your parents bear to let you go?

—They're gone. I live with my grandma. Do you think I'd make a good soldier?

—Your grandmother would miss you. The leaves are still falling; help me sweep up another pile. What happened to your parents?

Liu Ding took the broom. —I never knew them.

Old Zhao nodded. —I'm going fishing on Shadow Lake tomorrow morning.

—You're not supposed to do that! Shadow Lake has plenty of fish, but they're all poisonous. No one goes fishing there.

—Oh, really? I've caught fish there quite a few times.

—And you ate them?

—Yes, carp with long whiskers and a couple of little ones, all quite plump.

Liu Ding couldn't believe what he was hearing. —And nothing happened?

—They were pretty tasty, no muddy flavor. Why would they be poisonous? The water's so clear.

The smoke from the leaves was getting thicker and thicker, drifting across the field. Ever since Liu Ding was a little boy, he'd known to stay away from Shadow Lake and that the fish from there couldn't be eaten. He looked again at Old Zhao: long face, stubble outlining his mouth, the veins on his arm as clear as the markings on a leaf.

—What time?

—Six.

—Will you teach me to play the harmonica?

—Won't that scare the fish away?

—Maybe you'll feel like making some music after we're done fishing?

—Fine, and you bring something for us to eat.

Before bed that night, Grandma put new cotton padding in his winter trousers. The original stuffing had gone so flat, it looked like grilled fish when she pulled it out. He was wondering how to tell her he needed a packed lunch for the morning when she spoke.

—I have to head over to the west side tomorrow.

—What for?

—The last time I was down that way, old Mrs. Chong told me the Workers' Home to the north is now a sort of lecture hall. They're calling it Bright Hall—there's a man who gives speeches there.

—Speeches?

—Apparently he talks about God. Old Mrs. Chong had a stroke last year and her face got all twisted, but after listening to him talk, it's straightened up quite a lot.

—There's nothing wrong with you. Why do you need to listen?

—I might not be ill, but I'm old; it can't do any harm. I'll leave some food for you—I'll be home late.

Liu Ding wanted to ask about Shadow Lake—Grandma had spent half her life in this town, so she'd definitely know the answer—but he swallowed the words. He was terrible at lying, and if he opened his mouth, he was sure to let something slip about his outing with Old Zhao the next day. So he got his blanket from the cabinet and crawled onto the kang to sleep.

Grandma coughed, pulling Liu Ding out of his memory. He emerged from the kitchen to see Grandma putting her hair up. Usually, she just pushed it back haphazardly. Now she combed it carefully, revealing its salt-and-pepper sparseness, scraped it into a bun, and wrapped it in a little net. She retrieved a new pair of cloth shoes from the cabinet.

—Are you going to another talk?

Grandma reached under the mat for a little booklet.

—Not a talk, a sermon.

—You're a believer now? How much does it cost to listen?

—It doesn't cost money; you give as much as you like.

—So it does cost money.

—Silly boy, what do you know?

After the first sermon, she'd come back in tears, talking ceaselessly about Grandpa. Grandma never used to cry, but now it seemed she couldn't stop. Her tears spattered in all directions, flowing down her wrinkles onto her neck. She told him Grandpa was a team leader in the mine—when the shaft caved in, he stayed behind to rescue the others, and a second collapse killed him. He'd died without a single mark on his body, but his nose and mouth were filled with dirt. This was in 1972. Grandma said, We were stronger back then. We were all poor and miserable, but it was much more equal. When Grandpa was alive, he said to Grandma that if he became disabled, she'd have to take care of him and not abandon him, but if he died, he'd rest easy if she married someone else. Moved by these selfless words, Grandma never remarried—she brought up Liu Ding's mother all by herself.

—How old was my mother when it happened?

—Thirteen.

—That's how old I am now. Tell me about her.

—I don't want to talk about her; a fatherless child is never going to grow up properly.

Liu Ding might as well not have bothered asking. Grandma was extremely obstinate, and even after listening to the Lord, she still refused to divulge any more about his mother than she already had. He knew why: she didn't want him to go looking for her.

Grandma slipped her shoes on. The booklet in her hand seemed incredibly precious to her—she sat there leafing through it whenever she had any free time, after which it went back under the mat. She even brought it along when she went out to get groceries. Liu Ding had never read it. This didn't seem like a book—more like a talisman.

—I committed a sin today.

—When?

—In your principal's office. I let myself down. Anger and lying are both major sins.

—Wouldn't it have been a bigger sin if I'd been sent to reform school?

—But what if that was God's plan?

Liu Ding wondered what it would mean if God intended to send him to reform school. If that really was his plan, no wonder they didn't get along. This Lord was invisible, untouchable, and it was impossible to say what on earth he was thinking—he had to rely on this pastor to pass on his messages. Grandma said the pastor's name was Lin, and he knew all of God's thoughts—there was no question he couldn't answer. Liu Ding didn't know what a pastor did, but it sounded a bit like being a classroom cadre, passing on the teacher's thoughts and occasionally tattling on his fellows. When he'd been caught fighting before, Grandma had told Pastor Lin, who'd prayed for him. This had only increased Liu Ding's annoyance with the Lord and Pastor Lin. Bad enough having one person telling him what to do, and now suddenly here were two more, and both higher ranking than Grandma at that. Liu Ding thought that whether he ended up in the army or in Beijing, that was his own business, and he didn't want to obey the Lord. He resisted when Grandma tried to make him pray with her, but sometimes he failed and had to put on a show. Grandma shut her eyes, so he did, too. She didn't say anything, just silently communed with him. He didn't say anything either, and thought, Lord, if you're a decent person, just tell me where my mother is. At least give me a hint.

When he woke up on the morning of the fishing expedition, Grandma was already gone. On the table was the lunch she'd left for him: steamed buns and a heap of shredded cabbage mixed with chili oil. Liu Ding dug out the biggest lunch box he could find and stuffed it with two of the steamed buns and half the cabbage.

Shadow Lake was in the heart of Yanfen Street. Liu Ding had been there once as a kid, with Fatso and the others. He got a beating and never tried it again. All he remembered was a body of absolutely clear water large enough that you couldn't see all the way across, with a high cliff face on one side. Fatso, aged twelve at the time, shrugged off his clothes and climbed to the top of the cliff, then jumped into the lake. The other kids envied his boldness and swimming ability. A few days after that outing, Fatso came down with a high fever, and by the time he recovered, he had lost the ability to speak. Liu Ding still remembered Grandma's palm smacking into his face as soon as he stepped in the door. Right away she asked:

—Did you go into the water?

—No.

Another slap. —Did you go into the water?

—No, I swear, I didn't even go near the edge—only Fatso went in.

Grandma went into the storeroom and pulled out a large wooden basin. She gave him a bath in scalding, soapy water, then poured it away and filled it again, scrubbing him three or four times.

This time, Liu Ding arrived at Shadow Lake and found Old Zhao sitting on a little folding stool, bent over his fishing rod, earthworms wriggling in a tin can next to him. Only the pungent reek of tobacco from his rolled cigarette had a whiff of reality—the rest of the scene was like a dream. The autumn sun hadn't fully risen yet, and there was a chill in the air. The wind brushed past the withered grass at the edge of the lake and went right up into Liu Ding's shirt. The lake was as huge as ever, and the cliff face drifted in and out of view behind the morning mist. Faint ripples wrinkled the lake here and there, but mostly the water was calm, just like he remembered it. He really had been here—that childhood memory was genuine.

Old Zhao looked up. —There's another folding stool in that bag.

Liu Ding set it up next to him and sat there, staring out at Shadow Lake for quite a while.

—Did you bring food?

Liu Ding opened the lunch box. The buns had swelled up, squashing the cabbage to the edges. Old Zhao had a flask of very strong tea—the leaves came halfway up the side.

—Are there fish?

—Yes, but I haven't caught any yet.

A pause.

—Where are you from?

—The north.

—Were you really never in the army?

—No, why do you think I was?

—One time, I saw you brushing your teeth quickly.

—That's because I was in prison for nine years.

The rod twitched and Old Zhao turned the reel, but it slackened again. He cut an earthworm in two with a little blade, threaded half onto the hook, and put the other half back in the tin.

—Why were you in prison?

—I stabbed someone, for a friend.

—For a friend?

—The guy was strong, he didn't die, though I got him right in the heart. He just stood there, not even trying to duck— thought I wouldn't dare to stick the knife in. But my friend was good to me; he compensated the guy's family and got my sentence reduced. If he hadn't, I might not be alive now. He's in business now, in Beijing. He's asked me to join him, but I want to get some money together first to buy my way into his company—I don't want to be just a worker.

—In Beijing?

—Yes, Beijing. He wrote to me while I was locked up.

—Have you been to Beijing?

—A very long time ago.

—Have you seen a woman, about five foot five, square-faced? One of her ears is shriveled.

Old Zhao glanced at him. —No, I got the train there to see Chairman Mao; I didn't come across anyone like that.

—What was it like in prison? You still have a pair of hand-cuffs.

—That's the first thing I bought when I got out. I was

always getting cuffed while I was in there, and now I have a set of my own. My back was straight before, but whenever the guards didn't see eye to eye with me, they'd stick me into a cage that was too short to stand up straight and too narrow to sit down in. It ruined my back.

—Did you give in?

Old Zhao smiled. This was the first time Liu Ding had seen him smile, and for all his energetic brushing, his teeth were very yellow, and some were missing.

—I don't know what it means to give in. Decades ago, this country wasn't afraid of anyone. The Americans came, we beat them off. We were men, now we're boys. But you, you have to be a man. Hang on, I've got a bite.

A fat, dark-colored carp thrashed its tail as it rose from the water. Old Zhao used its momentum to arc it through the air onto the bank, smashing it against a rock and dropping it into the basket he'd set out in preparation.

They stayed very late that day and caught quite a few fish, big and little ones. When it grew colder, Old Zhao took his jacket off and draped it over Liu Ding's shoulders. They talked and talked. Liu Ding spoke about himself, and tried to explain about his mother, though he didn't know much and made up some of it. Old Zhao seemed to believe it all. Liu Ding said she was a very beautiful woman known to everyone in Yanfen Street who was so kind she always kept candy in her pockets for passing children, but then a bad man kidnapped her. He'd been trailing her for a long time, and then as soon as she had her baby, he spirited her away. Old Zhao said, It's not easy being a woman. He showed Liu Ding how to play the harmonica, and when Liu Ding didn't manage to produce a single note, he promised to continue the lesson another day. Then he played a tune that made Liu Ding want to cry, though he fought to keep the tears back. Old Zhao said the tune was called "Auld Lang Syne," and it was from a film in which a beautiful woman threw herself into the river out of shame. He saw it in prison. The woman really was lovely; she tilted her head to the side when she talked. One of the inmates couldn't accept that the film was over and got into a fight with a guard. Afterward, the prison said they weren't screening any more films.

—When you go to Beijing, can I come with you?

—What about your grandma? I can't bring both of you.

—I'll come back for her.

Old Zhao nodded. —I can tell that you don't fit in here. But let's be clear: you'll have to earn your keep, and looking for your mother is your own business.

—It's a deal, let's shake on it.

Old Zhao stretched out his hand, and so did Liu Ding. Old Zhao's hand was hard and icy cold, like a pair of pliers.

After that, Old Zhao took him on two more fishing trips. He'd saw a hole in the ice, let down a net, and catch a heap of fish in no time at all. Another day, Liu Ding wanted to see some trains, so Old Zhao brought him to the tracks. A green train came roaring by, with curtains the color of flesh. In the distance, two girls and a little boy stood by a snowman, watching. Old Zhao said:

—I used to hop trains, but you couldn't do that now.

—Do you think those passengers know that they're passing by Yanfen Street?

—Who knows? There isn't even a sign.

On the way home, Old Zhao began quietly singing.

The sun is in the west, the lake is still
I sing with joy and board the train
My metal steed, these tracks my killing fields
My blade slices through enemy hearts

In the present, the snow was starting again, coming down in dense, powdery drifts. Home alone, Liu Ding fed coal into the stove. There was a chill in his heart. What was the point of school? The kang toasted the insoles of his shoes, which lay there like dead fish. When they were dry, he slid them back into his shoes. He couldn't find his hat, but there was a leather cap in the kang cabinet, probably Grandpa's, and he put that on. It was loose and reeked of mothballs. He lifted the kang mat, and right at the far end, in a crack, he found a few expired ration coupons, which he left, and a couple of yuan, which he took. He got some paper and wrote: *Grandma, I've gone to look for my mother. I'll write again from Beijing. If you remember anything more about her, please tell me. I've already found a place to live. I'll come and get you when I'm settled. Liu Ding.* He read it over, then added: *Please ask your God to bless me.*

By the time he got to the school, his brows were filigreed with ice. He pushed open the gatehouse door. The lamp was off, and the only light came from the pale flickering of the stove. He stamped his feet and lifted the earflaps to shake off the snow. Only then did he notice Old Zhao on the single bed, a blanket over his body with his shoes sticking out.

—Are you asleep?

Old Zhao stirred.

—The school wants to keep me back a grade, so I need to borrow some money—I'm going to Beijing.

Old Zhao sat up against the wall. —Help me make a cigarette.

His cheeks were flushed red, his eyes were watery, and blisters marred his forehead. The loose tobacco and papers were on the shelf by the door. Liu Ding rolled a cigarette and handed it over.

—Don't get too close, I have chicken pox.

Liu Ding took a couple of steps back.

—I thought only children got that.

—Maybe it's because I never had it.

Liu Ding noticed a chunky fish tail in the tin lunch box by the stove, stiff and dark.

—I told you, you shouldn't have eaten those fish.

—It's nothing to do with the fish; I must have caught a chill. I was going to come see you today, I have some good news.

—What?

—We could have left for Beijing tonight—only I can't move now.

Liu Ding was so excited that, chicken pox or no, he took a step closer.

—How come?

Old Zhao took a drag on his cigarette, reached inside his woolen shirt, and pulled out two hundred yuan.

—Go to the long-distance station and get the bus to Shanhaiguan and change for the Beijing bus. When you arrive, find a phone booth and call this number. Ask for Manager Jiang—say you're a friend of Zhao Gexin. I'll come and find you there.

Liu Ding took the cash and the slip of paper.

—Where did the money come from?

—Don't ask, just go.

Liu Ding saw a wooden handle sticking out from under Old Zhao's pillow, and pulled—it was attached to a dagger, maybe a couple of handspans long, with a deep groove down the blade, which looked like it had just been sharpened.

—Tell me, or I'm not going. I'll just stand here and stare at you, and there's nothing you can do about it.

Old Zhao thought for a moment, and flung the cigarette butt on the ground.

—Someone asked me to sort something out.

—Sort something out?

—A person. One thousand yuan—two hundred up front, the rest when I finish the job.

—A person?

—A bad person. Seven years ago, he stabbed someone in the arm in Jiamusi. His victim survived at first, but died later. He's a wicked man—that wasn't the only bad thing he did. People wanted to kill him while he was in prison, but they didn't succeed.

—Is anyone really so evil?

—Many people. You can't see that because you're too young.

The fever made Old Zhao look much younger—his lips were reddened, as if he were wearing lipstick.

—What are you going to do?

—I was going to do it today. I heard that he's heading south tomorrow or the day after, but he's in Yanfen Street at the moment.

—He's here?

—Yes, his real name is Li, but he's going by Lin now. This isn't just about the money, you understand?

—Where does he live?

—I don't know, a different place every day, but he's supposed to be in Yanfen Street now. He's a pastor, and a lot of
people trust him, so he lives in their houses. Every Sunday,
he goes to the Workers' Home to speak. An illegal preacher. I
went to see him last week—he's a good talker. No wonder he's
taking people in.

Liu Ding started to feel suffocated—the gatehouse was
small, and the stove was blazing.

—What did he talk about?

—God, heaven, hell. He's not a true believer; otherwise he
wouldn't dare to talk about these things. He knows where he's
heading when he dies.

—Are you sure it's him?

—Yes, definitely, he has a tattoo on the back of his neck,
a small pair of wings. He went around with a box collecting
money, and I saw it then.

—But he's leaving tomorrow.

—Wherever he goes, I'll track him down.

—And if you can't, will you still come to Beijing?

—I'll find him, just like you'll find your mother.

—But how long will you keep looking?

—As long as it takes. I have to finish the job.

At that moment, Liu Ding felt completely alone, more
alone than he'd ever been. Even when he was a kid, when they
held him down and beat him up, he hadn't felt like this.

—He'll be there tonight? What time?

—Don't get involved.

—I've got the knife. I know who he is. You can't stop me,
so you might as well tell me everything.

Old Zhao tried to get up, but he was shivering all over, and all his strength was gone.

—You won't be able to do it.

—Then teach me.

Old Zhao tilted his head back and shut his eyes, as if talking had tired him out.

—We all choose our own paths in life. I have no regrets, but you might.

—When it's done, I'll leave on the bus. Come find me in Beijing when you're well again.

Old Zhao handed him the harmonica.

—He's speaking at seven tonight. Take this, and if Old Jiang doesn't believe you know me, just show this to him.

Next, he reached into his back pocket and passed Liu Ding the handcuffs and key.

—Only use these if you absolutely have to. Now, take the leather jacket hanging on the door.

Following his instructions, Liu Ding practiced stabbing the garment as if it were a man while Old Zhao called out:

—No, higher! Pull your arm back. You need to incapacitate him with that first hit.

—Okay, got it.

—When you're done, toss the knife into the grass, get as far away as you can, then get rid of the gloves, too.

Liu Ding imagined blood on the white ground, and then the falling snow covering it up.

—If you change your mind, throw the knife away and get on the bus. If you don't manage to kill him, just run, understand?

—How much is the bus ticket?

—Fifty yuan.

Liu Ding shoved the knife into his schoolbag, took a hundred yuan from the cash in his hand, and placed it on the shelf. Then he let down his earflaps and walked out the door.

3

The snow was getting heavier. Gooseberry's even breaths were in my ear, cooler now for the acetaminophen. I pinched her leg.

—Don't fall asleep.

She didn't reply.

—I'm going to get tired soon, you might have to carry me.

She lifted her head a little.

—Are you joking?

—Just look around—I've never seen a snowstorm this bad.

It was like steel curtains slamming down all around us. Only some of the streetlamps were on, leaving long stretches of darkness. The wind was rising too, like so many fingers tugging at my collar. The wind should be blowing northward, I thought. The landscape before us was becoming hazy.

—Is Pastor Lin dead? Did my mother leave? It's all blurry, like a dream—did it really happen?

I nodded.

—Where did Ma go?

—I don't know, but she'll be back.

—How do you know?

—Pastor Lin once said some people live to eat and sleep, while others live to find answers. Youngest Aunt will come back when she's found some answers.

—What do you mean, answers?

—I don't know how to explain it, but I'm sure they're worth looking for.

—To be honest, I always thought Ma would leave sooner or later—but I thought she would take me with her. And Pastor Lin? Did his soul go with her?

I thought about it.

—Probably. No, I mean definitely. Youngest Aunt said life's not going to be easy where she's going, and she didn't want you to suffer along with her. Bright Hall collapsed because of the snow, so we'll all meet again in my house soon.

A gigantic gust of wind swept the map out of my hand, and I couldn't see where it went. We're finished, I thought. Gooseberry had perked up and seemed to weigh less than she had a moment ago.

—Leave it, we can follow the streetlamps.

—I guess we'll have to.

After a while, she said my name.

—What?

—Look, is that a person?

I followed her pointing finger, and sure enough, someone was up ahead, hunched against the snow. Good, I thought, we can ask him for directions.

—Don't be scared, Gooseberry, I'm going to call to him.

—I'm not scared—go ahead and shout.

I gathered my nerve. —Hello?

The figure stopped.

—Where does this road go?

The figure suddenly started moving again, stumbling forward. His arm jerked and flung something away.

Gooseberry said: —What was that?

—I couldn't see.

The figure fell, picked himself up, and kept going, not even looking back.

—I guess I frightened him.

—I shouldn't have told you to shout, you were too loud. She sounded almost cheerful. Her neck craned.

—Go see what he threw.

—There's so much snow I can barely keep my eyes open. Why do you care about that?

—I think it went over there; I don't think he threw it very far.

—I'm almost out of strength. We'll freeze to death.

—It's there. I can see the handle.

I looked down and picked the object out of the snow by the side of the road. It was a dagger.

—I've got a flashlight in my bag. Here, you hold it.

Gooseberry shined the light at the blade, which was covered in blood. She shrieked.

—Don't be scared. That must be who stabbed Pastor Lin.

Gooseberry clutched my neck tight as she shoved the knife into my bag.

—What are you doing?

—I'm scared. It's making me sweat.

—If we keep following the streetlamps, they'll lead us out of here.

Even as I spoke, I was looking in the other direction, which was pitch-dark. I swept the flashlight across it, revealing a willow grove, into which the figure had disappeared.

—How long will the batteries last?

—Maybe two hours.

—Then shut up and chase him!

The snow was thicker among the willow trees, swallowing half my calves. My hands began to lose sensation, as if they were molded from plaster. Gooseberry had one arm around my neck and held the flashlight with the other hand. In the beam of light, snowflakes darted in all directions, and bare tree trunks reached straight up. I thought, What if he's turned back to the road? We'll be heading to our deaths. But if he really is so determined, and we catch up with him, that's suicide, too. Yet we kept going, maybe drawing courage from not being alone, or from the flashlight, or because we held in our hearts something of Pastor Lin, his voice raised as it was that evening: *When he summons us, we must answer, Here I am.* I didn't know which direction we were going in. What had Youngest Aunt said? *I have no home, and I have two legs; I can walk south.* The ice crystals on my eyelashes scraped every time I blinked. Snot ran from my nose and froze on my upper lip. Gooseberry kept turning the flashlight off to save power. When it blinked on again, I was shocked to see that we'd come out the other side of the forest onto a plain so smooth I thought I must be hallucinating. The wind had stopped, and the snow was falling straight down like rain. Then it started again and snowflakes spattered our faces. I stumbled, and Gooseberry said, Look.

The figure was ahead of us. The light swept across his heels. I gritted my teeth and pressed on. My feet almost slipped out from under me. He wasn't moving very fast. I saw him turn back to glance at us, then struggle to run a couple of paces. Gooseberry swung the flashlight around.

—What are you doing? Keep it on him.

—Something's wrong.

—What?

—There's a cliff over there. The ground is slippery as glass.

—So?

—I think we're on Shadow Lake.

I stopped walking and set her down. My arms had locked, and I had to lower them gingerly. My whole torso was numb with exhaustion, and tears were seeping from my eyes. Ahead of us, the figure still pressed on.

—Why have we stopped?

—I'm afraid we'll go through the ice.

—I won't, I'm lighter than you.

Gooseberry dashed ahead with the flashlight. I followed behind, calling at her to stop. The snow abruptly paused, and the wind calmed, too. Had it ceased everywhere, or just over Shadow Lake? Without the screen of snow, I could see that the figure was quite tall, wearing a leather cap with earflaps that swayed as he marched. He seemed completely drained. Gooseberry's footsteps were quick, and I couldn't keep up with her. She didn't seem to be tailing him so much as dancing across the ice. The figure turned, and warm breath spewed from his mouth. Gooseberry pointed the light in his eyes. Before I could tackle him, Gooseberry keeled over. I reached out to catch her, but my hand closed on air. One of her legs had broken through. She tried to pull herself free but succeeded only in shattering the ice around her. Half her body was now submerged. I heard splintering beneath me. She was just two steps away, but if I made a single move, we'd both go through. The figure reached out and grabbed Gooseberry. I called out that he should lie flat on the ice, and he said:

—Stop shouting!

Gooseberry said: —Did you kill Pastor Lin?

—Worry about yourself first. I'm going to pull you out, but then you'll have to stop chasing me.

—You did it, didn't you?

His face was already thawing out. Up close, he seemed about my age, a year or two older at most. A square face with round eyes, surprising for a young hooligan. He sat down on the ice and tried to haul Gooseberry out. She shrieked:

—Stop it!

—Do you want to die?

—I wasn't talking to you—someone's pulling my feet from below.

The ice around the hole disintegrated, and the two of them tumbled into the water. They sank rapidly, like chunks of metal, without a sound. Soon they were gone from view. The snow had stopped completely now, and so had the wind. I could hear myself breathing. The moon was visible. I thought about Youngest Aunt, a very strict person who would surely demand her daughter back eventually. I thought about my dad, but all that came to mind was drinking—his real family was booze. I took off my clothes and dove in.

In the underwater dark, shards of ice grated against my skin. My limbs began to stiffen, and the water stung my eyes, but I forced them to stay open, trying to spot Gooseberry Cold water pummeled me. My body slackened as my strength drained away. Warmth seeped from my spine into every inch of flesh. I shivered and felt a wash of sleepiness. Sinking. Sinking. All I felt was weight and exhaustion. I remembered lifting Gooseberry, and Youngest Aunt saying, Open up, open up. Hold her tight, said Youngest Aunt, don't let her fall. Something clutched at my legs, or maybe it was the current tugging at me. Stop that, I murmured. My own voice echoed. A door creaked open and shut on rusty hinges. Someone said, Do you confess? I said, Confess to what? The voice replied, Don't be stubborn. I said, I'm just telling the truth. It said, It would be better for you if you cooperated. I shouted, You're talking nonsense!

I opened my eyes to find myself behind a sheet of glass, all alone in a spartan room, lying on an iron bed next to a spittoon. Two words were embroidered in black on the pillowcase: *Zhang Mo.* How did they know my name? How long had this place been waiting for me? I touched my body—dry, no longer cold, in fact quite warm, though my arms still ached a little. Was this the bottom of Shadow Lake? I stood up from the bed and noticed the stench of piss. Three of the walls were stone, and on the other side of the glass was an enormous room, ten times larger than mine. A black coat and white scarf hung on a coatrack in one corner. In another stood a green safe, and in the middle of the room, a man in a pale gray suit sat at a desk. He wore glasses and a wide-brimmed hat with a dent in the crown. In front of him lay an ink pad, a stamp, and a stack of paper, on which he wrote with a fountain pen. Across from him, an empty chair. He licked his finger and flicked through the papers, shaking his head and muttering, Complete nonsense. After some time, he looked up and said, Next. A young man in a white shirt entered and sat down. He was bleeding from his nose onto his shirt, and kept fiddling with his long, greasy hair. He was young, eighteen or nineteen, and his every move and gesture reminded me of someone I knew. Whoever he turned those intense eyes on would feel they were about to hear words straight from his heart. Ah, I had it. It was Liao Chenghu.

GLASSES: Don't be stubborn.

LONG HAIR: I'm not, I just sculpt clay.

GLASSES: It would be better for you if you cooperated.

LONG HAIR: I haven't slept in two days. Just let me sleep a little.

GLASSES: You know what it is you sculpt?

LONG HAIR: Clay.

GLASSES: You sculpt poison! Have you ever made a likeness of the Chairman?

LONG HAIR: Other people make statues of the Chairman, but I'm not worthy.

GLASSES: Your family cut you off. Why don't you repent? You've been banished to Yanfen Street, and still you won't change your ways.

LONG HAIR: My family did the right thing, and I deserved to be banished. Please let me sleep, comrade.

GLASSES: Who did you sculpt?

LONG HAIR: A girl.

GLASSES: I'm asking you who.

LONG HAIR: I don't know who she was.

GLASSES: Nonsense. We've tracked her down. Her father's a rightist who got sent to the Yanfen coal mines. The two of you are setting up a rebel headquarters, aren't you?

LONG HAIR: No, I'm just a humble sculptor, and she was my model. There's no rebel headquarters.

GLASSES: Who is she to you?

LONG HAIR: I told you, I don't know her. I only saw her once.

GLASSES: Time and place.

LONG HAIR: The summer of 1970, beneath the banyan tree next to the Workers' Home.

GLASSES: What did you talk about?

LONG HAIR: We didn't talk. There was a group of rightist girls resting in the shade. They'd shaved her head, and her clothes were grimy. She was dancing under the tree. We were off to work. I took one look at her; then I had to hurry along.

GLASSES: Yet you managed to capture her exact likeness. Naked.

LONG HAIR: You're too kind.

GLASSES: Still so pleased with yourself. Don't you know where you are? Why not sculpt laborers or farmers or soldiers? Why this rightist's daughter?

LONG HAIR: I didn't know whose daughter she was. Her ears interested me—one of them looked odd. She seemed very innocent, oblivious to her surroundings. It was touching. And so I started imagining—I thought she would become a dancer one day. How old was she? Fifteen? Sixteen?

GLASSES: Answer the question: Why not sculpt laborers or farmers or soldiers?

LONG HAIR: I couldn't do it. Even when I tried, they came out crooked.

GLASSES: What you've just said condemns you to a lifetime of cleaning toilets. Where is it?

LONG HAIR: I threw it away.

GLASSES: The person who reported you said you hid it.

LONG HAIR: Where would I hide it? Old Gao must have seen wrongly.

GLASSES: Where did you dump it?

LONG HAIR: In Shadow Lake.

GLASSES: Nonsense, you couldn't have done that.

LONG HAIR: I told you, it's in Shadow Lake. Feel free to drag the water. You might find some dead bodies, too—quite a few people drowned themselves recently. They're probably just bones by now.

Glasses leaned back in his chair and stared at him.

GLASSES: I'll be frank. You're still young, and you could make something of yourself in the future. But if you keep resisting, your body will suffer. There's been a recommendation that I bring you into a struggle session and cut off your fingers so you can never sculpt again. Tell me where the figurine is—I'll be able to answer to my superiors, and you'll avoid torture. I have nothing against you; I'm just defending Chairman Mao. Think about it.

Long Hair was quiet for a while.

LONG HAIR: I made this figurine for myself. No one else had the right to look at it, so I threw it away. You're protecting Chairman Mao, but I also have people to protect. Life is long, and judgment doesn't happen right away— someday, you may look back and think none of this was necessary. Fish don't have to eat flesh—they can live on water, too.

Glasses put the cap back on his pen and looked at Long Hair.

GLASSES: I see. Fingerprint, please.

I banged on the glass and screamed, I know where the clay figurine is! It seemed they couldn't see or hear me. Long Hair stood and pressed his fingertip into the ink pad. The fingernail was very long. He stamped his finger on the paper and immediately shrank to the size of a handspan, even smaller than the clay figurine. He seemed dazed as he gazed up at the table leg. Glasses reached down to pick him up, and locked him in the safe along with his written report.

He returned to his seat, unscrewed the bottom of his fountain pen, and topped up the ink. Then he called in the next person.

This man was badly hunched over, and wrinkles lined his face. He wore a yellow singlet and was in handcuffs.

GLASSES: Sit.

Handcuffs sat.

GLASSES: Name?

HANDCUFFS: Zhao Gexin.

GLASSES: Age?

HANDCUFFS: Thirty-five.

GLASSES: Do you know why you're here?

HANDCUFFS: Yes, I stabbed a man.

GLASSES: Did you know there's a crackdown on illegal activity?

HANDCUFFS: It was an accident.

GLASSES: You stabbed a man in the heart by accident?

HANDCUFFS: We exchanged words, and I got worked up.

GLASSES: How many times have you been in here?

HANDCUFFS: This is my third time. I haven't slept in two days. Please let me sleep a little.

GLASSES: And all these times were because of that man Jiang?

HANDCUFFS: No, they were my own business.

GLASSES: Nonsense. You didn't know any of these people.

HANDCUFFS: We had words.

GLASSES: Just tell us about Jiang, and you can go straight to sleep. Don't be stupid.

HANDCUFFS: This doesn't concern Jiang. He's a businessman, and I'm the scum of the earth. We have nothing to do with each other.

GLASSES: When you were both Red Guards, weren't you in the same company?

HANDCUFFS: That was a long time ago.

GLASSES: I know it was a long time ago. Things are different now. People have died, and someone needs to pay.

HANDCUFFS: My brain is like glue. Please let me sleep.

GLASSES: Tell me how Jiang gave you orders.

HANDCUFFS: He didn't give me orders. I just don't know my own strength. I can't control myself.

GLASSES: Do you know what will happen if you stick to this story?

HANDCUFFS: I do, but I'm telling the truth.

GLASSES: If you insist, do you know what will happen to your parents?

HANDCUFFS: I've hit my dad and cut myself off from him. Now they've disowned me, too. I've been in prison twice before, and no one came to visit.

GLASSES: You have to take responsibility.

HANDCUFFS: I've said everything I could possibly say, please let me sleep.

Glasses leaned back in his chair.

GLASSES: Fingerprint, please.

The same thing happened again: he abruptly shrank. The little man scurried under the chair, but Glasses grabbed him by the collar and put him in the safe.

Belatedly, I realized my room had no door. Maybe they would come and interrogate me eventually. But what would they ask? Maybe where the clay figurine was, though I wasn't sure how much they actually cared about that. For some reason, I got the sense that Glasses was just toying with us. I studied the walls of the big room, trying to spot any gaps I could flee into once I'd shrunk—but they were pristine, as if newly built.

Glasses took off his hat and ran a hand through his hair. Though he looked middle-aged, his hair was completely white. He rubbed his forehead and put the hat back on. Now the young hooligan and Gooseberry walked in. I pressed my face to the glass.

Glasses fetched another chair from a corner of the room.

GLASSES: Sit.

They sat. Gooseberry's legs dangled in the air.

GLASSES: What's the problem? Tell me in your own words.

Both of them remained silent.

GLASSES: Don't waste my time. There are people waiting to
come in after you. Speak.

HOOLIGAN: I don't know where we are or why we're here.

GLASSES: (*to Gooseberry*) Do you?

GOOSEBERRY: I fell through the hole in the ice and got dragged
under.

Glasses picked up his pen.

GLASSES: Time and place.

GOOSEBERRY: Middle of the night, Shadow Lake.

GLASSES: Year and date.

GOOSEBERRY: Nineteen ninety-three. I don't remember the
date. Sunday.

GLASSES: Tell me about your case.

HOOLIGAN: Let us go, I have stuff to do.

GLASSES: What stuff?

HOOLIGAN: I don't need to tell you.

GLASSES: Going to find your mother?

The hooligan's face tensed.

HOOLIGAN: You spoke to my principal?

GOOSEBERRY: (*to Hooligan*) My mother's missing, too.

GLASSES: We'll discuss that later. Liu Ding, tell me about your case.

HOOLIGAN: Do you know where my mother is?

GLASSES: Maybe I do, maybe I don't, but I am in charge of your case. I've got the file here.

HOOLIGAN: What file?

GLASSES: Had the pastor done something to hurt you?

HOOLIGAN: I don't know any pastors.

GLASSES: How do you know Zhao Gexin?

HOOLIGAN: Why are you asking me questions?

GLASSES: All you need to know is that I'm always right.

The hooligan stood and threw a punch. His fist hit Glasses's chin and kept going, right through his face, leaving the hooligan sprawled across the table.

GLASSES: Sit back down. How do you know Zhao Gexin?

HOOLIGAN: What are you? A shadow?

GLASSES: How do you know Zhao Gexin?

HOOLIGAN: (*glaring*) He's the ethics teacher at my school. And my friend.

GLASSES: Did he send you after the pastor?

HOOLIGAN: No, I went fishing with him.

GLASSES: Just tell the truth. The faster we get through this, the sooner this little girl can leave.

Gooseberry played with her plait.

HOOLIGAN: This has nothing to do with her.

GLASSES: Yes, it does. If not for you, she wouldn't be here.

GOOSEBERRY: Did you stab Pastor Lin?

HOOLIGAN: That's how she's involved? She knows the pastor?

GLASSES: What more do you need? Let me be clear: now that you're here, you're not leaving. It's no longer any of your business where your mother is, because you'll never find her. But if you come clean, you'll suffer a little less, and the girl can go free.

HOOLIGAN: I don't know her at all—you think you can get to me by threatening her?

GLASSES: Listen. In some place you can't see, this little girl is choking on water. Her body is growing cold, her clothes are getting heavier, and soon she'll sink to the bottom of the lake. There's a little boy with her—the same thing will happen to him.

GOOSEBERRY: My cousin's here, too?

GLASSES: He jumped in after you. Thinks he's some kind of hero.

HOOLIGAN: He looked like an idiot.

GOOSEBERRY: My cousin's not an idiot. Did you do it?

HOOLIGAN: Where did your mother go?

GOOSEBERRY: She left because Pastor Lin died, I don't know where to.

HOOLIGAN: You're better off than me. I've never met mine.

GOOSEBERRY: Why did you stab Pastor Lin?

HOOLIGAN: I wanted to leave, so I could find my mother. I wanted Old Zhao to come with me. Maybe I wasn't thinking straight.

Gooseberry stared at him for quite a while.

GOOSEBERRY: Are you going to become a better person?

HOOLIGAN: I don't know. As soon as I did it, I knew I shouldn't have. Maybe it was the blizzard—everything was blurry. If it hadn't been snowing, I might have seen things more clearly.

GLASSES: Did Zhao Gexin tell you what to do?

HOOLIGAN: What's my father's name?

GLASSES: I don't know.

HOOLIGAN: What's my real surname?

GLASSES: I don't know. Answer the question. Did Zhao Gexin give you an order?

HOOLIGAN: Is my mother alive? Is she doing well? Does she have more children? Do I have a little brother or sister?

GLASSES: I don't know. Hurry up, this little girl and her cousin are sinking.

HOOLIGAN: He didn't tell me what to do. He mentioned the job, but I was the one who decided to do it. He tried to stop me.

GLASSES: Is that the truth?

HOOLIGAN: Yes.

GLASSES: Do you know this man Jiang?

HOOLIGAN: No. Old Zhao mentioned him, and after the job was done we would meet in Beijing.

GLASSES: You wouldn't have met. The phone number and address Old Zhao gave you are out of date.

HOOLIGAN: That's not possible.

GLASSES: Jiang has abandoned Zhao Gexin, but Zhao Gexin hasn't accepted this. No one wanted Pastor Lin dead. All the stories about him, Zhao Gexin gleaned from listening to his sermons. He wanted Pastor Lin dead because Lin had been granted mercy.

The hooligan was silent for a few seconds.

HOOLIGAN: Old Zhao's my friend. I believe him, not you.

GLASSES: Fine. Last question: Can you identify him?

HOOLIGAN: I'm not getting out of here, am I?

GLASSES: No, you're already at the bottom of the lake.

HOOLIGAN: If the girl gets out, will she find her family?

GLASSES: You don't need to worry about that.

HOOLIGAN: If you know where my mother is, please tell me. I'm begging you.

GLASSES: Will you identify him?

The hooligan nodded.

HOOLIGAN: (*to Gooseberry*) Forgive me, kid? It's because the snow was so heavy. I know it was.

Gooseberry adjusted her plait and said nothing.

HOOLIGAN: Will you forgive me?

Gooseberry looked up.

GOOSEBERRY: What does your mother look like?

HOOLIGAN: Very beautiful. Square face, slim body, long hair. One of her ears is a bit twisted up, but she's still good-looking.

GOOSEBERRY: I feel like I've seen her, but I don't know where.

GLASSES: Fingerprint, please.

HOOLIGAN: (*to Gooseberry*) I've never seen her, but if you find her, tell her I never forgot her. Her scent is still on me. I never drank her milk, but I know what kind of person she is. I know she didn't want to leave me—there must have been some reason she couldn't stay to see me grow up.

The hooligan reached for the ink pad.

GOOSEBERRY: Don't do it.

GLASSES: Now what?

GOOSEBERRY: What's going to happen to him?

GLASSES: His time is up.

GOOSEBERRY: I don't think so. He's leaving with me.

Gooseberry turned to the hooligan.

GOOSEBERRY: Go look for your mother yourself. I can't do it for you.

GLASSES: Are you deaf? Didn't you hear what I said? Your lungs are already half full of water. You're going to drown in a few seconds.

GOOSEBERRY: Why should I listen to you?

GLASSES: I'm in charge here. Haven't you noticed?

GOOSEBERRY: I only listen to my mother and my cousin. Well, I half-listen to him. Who do you think you are? You said you're always right. Pastor Lin told us that the least trustworthy people are the ones who think they're free of sin.

Glasses put his papers into a stack and tapped the sides to straighten them.

GLASSES: Fine, then we'll end here. No problem.

HOOLIGAN: (*to Gooseberry*) You should go. This is between me and him. This guy's a shadow. Can't you hear? When he speaks, there's no echo.

Gooseberry pulled out my flashlight.

GOOSEBERRY: I think the batteries still work.

She turned the beam on Glasses, which made him shiver.

GLASSES: Turn it off!

GOOSEBERRY: Who are you to bully us?

Glasses shook his head so violently, his hat fell to the ground. The light shone through his clothes, and underneath were fish scales.

Now his glasses and clothes were gone, revealing the body of an enormous fish, its tail like an anchor, three pairs of black fins on its back. A couple of withered claws protruded from its chest, holding the report it had just written. The creature emitted a high-pitched cry, as if a hook had pierced its jaw.

The hooligan grabbed hold of a fin.

All of a sudden, water surged in, sweeping up Gooseberry and the hooligan. The glass wall vanished—the iron bed sank beneath the waves, and the flood caught me, too. I swam as hard as I could toward Gooseberry. Still clutching the documents, the fish tried to reach the safe, but the hooligan wouldn't release its fin, and Gooseberry gripped its tail. I managed to grab Gooseberry's ankle, the ankle that Youngest Aunt had beaten so many times. The fish thrashed from side to side but couldn't shake us off. It twisted around and bit the boy. Its teeth were jagged, like broken glass, and sank into his left side. He shuddered, and blood poured from him. He reached into a pocket, brought out a pair of handcuffs, and snapped one bracelet around his own wrist, while using the other to pierce the fin, which oozed black blood. He gestured to us that we should let go, but Gooseberry refused. She hooked her little hands onto the scales of its tail. The fish arched its body and pushed the safe ahead of it. I felt the water crushing my chest with its immense weight. At the bottom of the lake, there was a hole that the water was spiraling toward, grains of sand swirling around and around. The giant fish tossed the safe into the hole and tried to follow, but the hooligan twisted around and blocked him. The fish bit him in the chest and pushed him out of the way. I realized my feet were touching mud, so I dug in my heels and pulled at the fish. Suddenly it had a neck and protruding eyes. Its jaw stretched out to bite Gooseberry, but I pulled her aside, and its teeth closed on water. I saw a crazed panic in its gaze, as if it would die if it didn't get inside the hole. In a single bite, it severed its own tail, sending Gooseberry and me flying. I threw my arms around her and watched as the hooligan clung tightly to the fish, handcuffs glittering in the water. He shot us one last look. The half of the fish's body he was attached to dragged him into the hole, a bone poking out where its tail used to be, like a broken tree branch. Soon it had disappeared, and moments later the hole was blocked by sludge. I started to choke. Holding Gooseberry, I swam upward. There was no more oxygen. I spat out a mouthful of water and breathed in some more.

A sparrow landed on my face. I opened my eyes, but it had already leaped away, and was darting nimbly across the snowy ground. My legs were half in flowing water. I turned my head and saw Gooseberry lying by my side, trying to sit up. Beyond the withered grass was Shadow Lake, covered in a sheet of ice. There must be an underwater current that let out here, I figured, warm enough to remain unfrozen. I'd grown up here, but somehow I hadn't known this rivulet existed.

Gooseberry looked at me. —We're out?

—Seems so.

—Did the fish get away, too?

—Yes, but it was half-dead.

—Did the big guy manage to escape?

We looked around for a while. The sparrow flew away, leaving no sign that it had ever been there. Shadow Lake was covered with snow, perfectly smooth, without a single footprint.

Gooseberry asked: —Do you think he could have come up somewhere else?

—Who knows how wide Shadow Lake is. Maybe he swam away; maybe he dragged the fish onto land and it's drying out now. He seemed strong, that kid.

—I feel like he asked me to do something, but I don't remember what. Where's the clay figurine I kept in the attic?

—Still at Bright Hall—we didn't bring it with us.

—It was really lovely. Do you think we'll be able to find it?

—It must be somewhere; it can't have vanished.

Gooseberry began to cry, soaking my sleeve with her tears.

—Bright Hall collapsed, and my mother's gone. Do you think we'll be able to bring her back?

—Yes. It's hard to walk away, and easy to come back.

—The big guy's mother was never found.

—Youngest Aunt is different. She'll have a plan.

—What will she eat out there, without the refectory?

—There's a world of restaurants, with better food.

—Will she forget me?

—Not possible. She had the Bible in her pocket, and every time she reads it, she'll think of you.

Gooseberry gradually stopped crying. The sun was high in the sky, illuminating the pure white snow on the branches. Nothing but snow and sun and wind.

—Can you hear my stomach growling?

—I'll cook you noodles when we get home.

—You know how to cook noodles?

—It's my specialty.

The snow had stopped, and the sky was clear. It felt as if there were no one in Yanfen Street except the two of us. To be honest, I'd never cooked noodles before, but I thought I'd give it a try—it couldn't be that difficult. And maybe we'd step through the doorway and see my father lounging on the kang, fast asleep by the heat of the stove. So I'd make three bowls of noodles, each topped with an egg and chopped scallions. The path ahead was very straight. I took Gooseberry's hand, and we skirted the shore of the lake, walking in the direction of home.

MOSES ON THE PLAIN

ZHUANG DEZENG

In 1995, I formally left the municipal tobacco plant and went into business for myself, heading south to Yunnan with an accountant and salesman in tow. During the Cultural Revolution, I'd only reached middle school when I was sent down to the countryside, like most Educated Youths. When I finally got back to Shenyang, I took over my father's position in the cigarette distribution department, where there wasn't actually any work to do. There were only three of us, and we spent our days reading the papers and drinking tea. I was young, male, and distantly related to the plant manager, so I was promoted to department head a few years later. Several years my senior, both of my subordinates called me Young Zhuang rather than "boss."

Then I was introduced to Fu Dongxin. A fellow returned Educated Youth, she was twenty-seven at the time, and not bad-looking at all, with her long black hair and ramrod-straight back. A bit on the short side, but she had a soothing personality and was always even-tempered. Her father used to be a professor at our local university—he taught philosophy, which I know nothing about. I heard he fraternized with the idealist faction and was brought down during the anti-rightist movement. His students incinerated much of his book collection and took the rest to paste over cracks in their windows. He was beaten up during the Cultural Revolution, leaving him deaf in one ear. By the time he regained his position, he was unable to teach. His three children—Fu Dongxin was the middle one—worked at the factory. Not one of them followed him into academia, and all married into the working class.

The first time I met Fu Dongxin, she asked what books I'd read. The only thing I could dredge up from my memory was a cartoon version of *Dream of the Red Chamber* that a classmate had lent me before I was sent down. She asked if I still knew the main character's name, and I said all I remembered was a girl who cried all the time and a sissified guy. She laughed and allowed that this was a pretty good summary. Then she asked about my hobbies, and I said I liked swimming: the Hun River in summer, and in the winter, the Beiling Park artificial lake, which was where we were at that very moment, in a rowboat. It was the fall of 1980, and though the frost hadn't come yet, temperatures were dropping sharply. I was wearing a turtleneck sweater my mother had knitted for me, under a black leather jacket I'd borrowed from a friend. She was sitting across from me in a red scarf and black cloth shoes. At her age Dongxin was considered an old maid, an ordinary worker who left the factory each day stinking of tobacco, the same as everyone else. Yet just then, she looked as fresh-faced as a student on an autumn outing. She told me the book she was holding, which was by a Russian, contained a really well-written short story called "The District Doctor"; she'd finished reading it on the bus here.

—Do you know it?

—No.

—A woman is drowning, so a man takes off his clothes and dives in to rescue her. She grips his neck and they head to shore, but she's swallowed too much water and knows she's done for. When she looks at the back of his neck—the fine hairs, the tendons protruding because of his exertions—she falls in love with him just before dying. Do you believe this sort of thing can happen?

—I'm a good swimmer; you don't need to worry.

She laughed again. —You've come along at the right time. I know you're not sophisticated, but the one book you've read as a comic is a great novel. As long as you don't look down on me and my foolish refinement, we'll get along.

—I sound stupid now, but I'm not normally like this.

— I know, the matchmaker said you were a leading figure among the Educated Youths. You made quite a name for yourself.

—If there's food to be had in this world, I'll find it and make sure you eat the best of everything, not just leftovers.

—In the evenings, when I'm reading or writing in my journal, I don't like to be disturbed.

—Will we sleep together?

She didn't answer, just indicated that I should keep rowing, all the way back to shore.

A year into our marriage, Zhuang Shu was born. Dongxin chose the name. Till he was three, I picked him up every day

from the factory day care while she went grocery shopping
and made dinner—division of labor. Actually, there was no
choice. Her cooking was dreadful, but it would have been
reckless to put her in charge of the kid. One time, Shu's foot
got caught in his stroller and she didn't notice, just wondered
why it wasn't moving and yanked harder. She wasn't popu-
lar at the factory—she neither played cards nor knitted, and
she spent her lunch breaks reading a book among the piles of
tobacco leaves. Naturally, she drifted apart from her cowork-
ers. Although the atmosphere had thawed since the early
eighties, people still had plenty of opinions about the likes
of her, and if the revolution returned, she'd be the first to get
denounced. Once I joined her for lunch, and her packed meal
was cold. Apparently this had been going on for some time—
she'd put her lunch box in the steamer drawer every morning,
but someone would remove it. I went to talk to her manager,
who said he couldn't do anything about interpersonal con-
flicts; it's not like he was a police officer or anything. Then he
complained that everyone on her shift had to do extra labor
because she worked so slowly, as if this were embroidery, and
said that when a study group convened to discuss Comrade
Deng Xiaoping's words, she drew a picture of Deng in her
notebook instead, making him the size of the town gate, with
Comrades Hua Guofeng and Hu Yaobang tiny as toys. He
didn't want to embarrass me, or he'd have spoken to management long ago and had her transferred to a different department. In a burst of inspiration, I hurried to the nearest store for
two bottles of Western Phoenix liquor, put them on his desk,
and said, Transfer her to the print room.

Since childhood, Fu Dongxin had copied illustrations
from her picture books, and on our wedding day, part of her

trousseau was a collection of these drawings. They were quite something—a guy with a hump ringing the bells on the roof of a huge cathedral and a foreign-looking girl in a big dress. She'd drawn the pleats on the skirt in so much detail, I could almost hear them rustle. The day I spoke to her manager, after dinner, I took a stool out into the courtyard to enjoy the cool air while she reclined on the bed, reading, and Shu sat nearby playing with a box of matches, rattling it by his ear or holding it up to his nose and sniffing. We had a black-and-white TV set but rarely turned it on, for fear of disturbing her. After a while, Dongxin brought a stool out too, sat beside me, and said:

—I'm moving to the print room tomorrow.

—Good. That's easier work.

—I spoke to the supervisor today and offered to illustrate a few cigarette packets, in case they wanted to use them.

—Draw away.

She thought for a moment. —Thank you, Dezeng.

I didn't know what to say, so I just smiled. That's when Li came by with his daughter, Fei. There were more than twenty houses in our row, and Li had the one at the east end. He was a bench worker at the tractor factory. Square face, medium height, sturdy build. I'd known him since we were kids. He was the youngest of three, but both his brothers feared him. He'd amassed a valuable collection of commemorative stamps during the Cultural Revolution, never mind that he'd had to injure quite a few people to get hold of them. We'd fought too, but afterward we both forgot about it. He became a lot steadier after getting married. Good with his hands and able to swallow hardship, he was destined to get ahead. His wife also used to be at the tractor factory, a spray painter who wore a mask at all times, which left a pale square around her nose and mouth. Unfortunately, she'd died giving birth to Fei. Li looked at the three of us and said:

—Look at you, sitting all in a line. Are you in class?

I smiled. —Taking Fei for a walk?

—She wanted an ice pop, so we went to buy one from old Mrs. Gao.

Meanwhile, Fei and Shu were negotiating—she wanted to trade half her popsicle for his box of matches. He glanced at Dongxin, who said:

—Go on, Shu, give the matches to Fei, but don't take the popsicle.

No sooner had she uttered the words when Shu tossed the matchbox to the ground and snatched the popsicle out of Fei's hand. Fei picked up the matches, lit one, and stared at the flame. The night was dark and moonless. When the matchstick was halfway gone, she used it to light the box. Li rushed forward to grab it, but it was already blazing away. Very deliberately, she flung the fireball into the air—not because it was burning her hand, but just for the hell of it. It sizzled as it rocketed above us. She'd thrown it high.

JIANG BUFAN

After I got redeployed from the army, I worked on a few cases involving the many anti-crime campaigns. We nabbed plenty of people—nothing too serious, just held them overnight and made them sweat a bit. Petty thieves and low-level criminals, which was all I'd expected to find in a backwater like Shenyang.

Then the Two Wangs arrived on the scene. Big Wang had

been roughed up during the crackdowns, and Little Wang had spent some time in the army, not far from where I'd been bivouacked in eastern Inner Mongolia, where he'd gained a reputation as a sharpshooter who could change magazines with one hand. Held the record for speed. The Wangs robbed a string of savings banks and jewelers, armed with a handgun each and over a thousand bullets, every one of which had been smuggled out of the army by Little Wang and sent to his brother. It's hard to imagine it now, five bullets crammed into the envelope with each letter home. Soon the city's entire police force was after them, and the streets were plastered with their "Wanted" posters. They strapped bars of gold and cash to themselves but had nothing to eat, so they began to break into private homes; they'd tie up the occupants, head to the kitchen to cook themselves a meal, then rush out. They never hurt anyone much, and sometimes they even left money for the food. Later still, they tossed the cash and jewelry into the river and returned fire against the police, so we switched to plain clothes to avoid becoming targets. Finally, that winter, we cornered them on Chessboard Hill, to the north of the city. I was stationed at the foot of the slope, rifle over my chest, gripping it with the sleeves of my army greatcoat pulled over my hands. Never mind a human being—if a deer had come past, I would have fired at it. Then the news filtered down that the criminals had been shot dead. I didn't see the bodies, but I heard that the pair of them were scrawny as starving dogs, sprawled in the snow in their unlined clothes. To be accurate, Big Wang was shot dead, and Little Wang shot himself. That night, I went home and got blind drunk. The whole experience had been a lot more than I'd bargained for, but after much serious thought, I convinced myself to stay in the force.

At the start of the winter of 1995, five local taxi drivers were killed in the span of a month. Their bodies were left in their cars, which were dumped in the wilderness on the edge of the city and burned beyond recognition. It would have been six deaths, except the last driver was extra vigilant because one of the victims had been from his firm. He picked up a man one night and sensed that something was wrong. Halfway to their destination, he fled from the car and hid in the woods. He said his passenger was of medium build and fortyish, with a square face and large eyes. He couldn't confirm that this was the murderer—he'd watched from the trees as the man got out and walked away, without touching any of the cash in the vehicle.

This streak of murders caused quite a stir, though the higher-ups suppressed the numbers and the newspapers reported only two dead, one missing. I made a pledge to my commanders that I would solve the case within twenty days. Then I called a meeting at my house with several figures from the underworld and told them that the person who handed over the killer would be my sworn brother from then on. We'd eat from the same pot and drink from the same bowl. No one took me up on that—they genuinely had no idea, which meant it wasn't a gangster but some civilian going rogue. I checked out the histories of those five drivers, but they weren't connected in any way: an official's chauffeur, an army driver, someone who'd lost his factory job and sold his house to live in rented rooms so he could afford a license. I scoured the burnt vehicles and found shreds of nylon rope. The killer must have strangled the drivers, taken their money, driven the taxis to a deserted area, poured gasoline over them, and set them alight. There were several clues here: the killer was strong, knew how to drive, and needed quick cash. The cars were worth far more than the small amounts of money he took, of course, but either he knew he wouldn't be able to sell them or he didn't have time. Five cases in one month—no one would take such a big risk unless they were desperate. I had a meeting with the guys in forensics, who said the gas tank alone wouldn't have been enough to cause such an inferno—the killer must have brought his own fuel. Another clue.

Ten days passed with no breakthrough. I entered my commander's office, sat down, and said:

—This won't be easy to crack.

—What do you need, money or manpower? There's a lot of pressure from the top brass—only half as many drivers dare to go out at night now, and people are having trouble getting cabs. Solve this and I'll do everything in my power to get you promoted.

—Sir, being a police officer feels like wiping other people's asses.

—What do you mean by that?

—Never mind. Just tell the higher-ups that every cab in the city needs a protective screen around the driver's seat. Our guy is a strangler, and even if he has other methods, it won't be firearms, so this ought to keep everyone ninety percent safe, not just from this killer but from any future copycats. It's essential.

—That's expensive—I'm not sure it will be approved.

—Lately the streets have been full of workers who've lost their jobs and become desperate. Remember the one we caught not long ago? He would hide inside building entrances and bash people's heads in with an ax, sometimes for as little as five yuan. Just take the crime scene photos with you when you go in, show them brains oozing from heads and charred bones.

—I'll find a way to convince them. Let's get back to what you need.

—I've got six people on my team, but one can't drive. Find me five cars, and I'll send them out tonight without protective screens.

I summoned my subordinates and warned them: —There's some risk involved in this, so feel free to drop out. If you succeed, there'll be a reward as well as kudos, but if you fail, you might end up like those five drivers, burned to a crisp. Think about it.

Mo Xiaodong said: —Sir, how much of a reward?

I knew his wife was pregnant, and he hadn't been home much in the last couple of weeks. He was the one I was most afraid would say no.

—The reward isn't fixed, but it should be more than five thousand yuan, to be shared among the group.

He nodded and fell silent.

Around ten-thirty p.m. on December 16, 1995, the five of us set off in our cars. Each of us had two guns, one in an underarm holster, one hidden under the driver's seat. I told the men to look out for a few things: first, one or more middle-aged men asking to be taken to a remote location; second, a lone middle-aged man choosing to sit right behind the driver's seat; third, anyone smelling of gas or kerosene. If you're hailed by a woman or anyone with a kid, say you're new and don't know the way. Finally, if it comes to a fight, don't hold back—we're talking about a murderer here, and it's his life or yours.

The next three days were uneventful. Xiaodong said he'd picked up three suspicious-looking men with local accents who wanted to go as far away as Su Village, which put him on alert. Halfway there, one of them asked to stop so he could piss. Xiaodong pulled the gun from under his seat and stuck it into his padded boot. Then the pissing guy returned, and the three men kept talking. Turns out they were brothers on their way home for their dad's burial—one of them had taken a girl to a bar beforehand; hence the full bladder. They arrived at Su Village to find the funeral tent already set up. Xiaodong lit a cigarette and watched as the other two brothers helped the drunk one in. They knelt to pay their respects, while Xiaodong got back in the car and drove off.

Around ten-thirty p.m. on December 24, the ninth day of our operation, it started snowing a little. I parked at the corner of Nanjing and North Third, cracked a window, had a smoke, then settled in for a nap. All of us were sleeping in fits and starts, grabbing some shut-eye whenever we felt too tired to go on. From a nearby dance hall, I could hear a faint carol, something about sleigh bells ringing. The car in front of me picked up a middle-aged woman in a mink coat. I nudged my vehicle ahead, flicked away the cigarette butt, and rolled up the window. Two people emerged from the alleyway at the south end of the dance hall: a middle-aged man and a girl of twelve or thirteen. He had a square face and a medium build, and both hands were stuck in the pockets of his black leather jacket, which was cracked and limp as an old rag. The girl was wearing a white surgical mask, blue trousers that looked like part of a school uniform, and a red padded jacket obviously meant for an adult—it reached down to her knees.

She also had a pink schoolbag, its strap dark from use. Snowflakes dotted her hair.

The man came over and rapped on my window. —You free?

I waved him away. —I'm going off shift soon.

—My girl's stomach hurts, and we need to get to the Chinese clinic in Yanfen Street.

—You ought to take her to the hospital.

—The hospital's expensive, and this traditional doctor's excellent; he cured me before, and he's good with women's cramps.

I thought about it. —I don't know the way. You'll have to guide me.

—Fine.

He slid into the seat right behind me. The girl took the passenger seat, holding her schoolbag in her lap.

Yanfen Street was a shantytown at the easternmost end of the city, just before it turned into farmland. As it happened, that was where I often ended up arresting people.

The man's hands remained in his pockets, and his ears were red with cold. The girl kept her eyes shut and tipped her head back, clutching the bag to her stomach. We drove on. He gave me plenty of warning before each turn. After a while, I asked, Do you have a cigarette? He fished one out of his pocket and handed it over.

—What line of work are you in?

—I used to work in a factory; now I'm a small businessman.

—Factories are closing down everywhere.

—Some are doing all right. 601 Institute is fine, for instance.

—The airplane workshop?

—Yes, places like that are thriving.

—What kind of business are you in?

He met my gaze in the rearview mirror. —Just a bit of buying and selling. I've tried quite a few things.

—And your wife?

—Turn right up ahead, then straight.

It looked like we were going past Yanfen Street. The girl's eyes remained shut, and she was perfectly still. The man stared out the window, apparently unwilling to continue the conversation. I said:

—It's not easy to do anything now.

He grunted.

—Being a cab driver, I see police everywhere during the day—it's hard to get around. You can go faster at night, but I'm afraid of being robbed.

—It's not that bad.

—Haven't you seen the news? Five drivers were killed recently.

He looked in the mirror again. —Did they catch him?

—No, that won't be easy; he's a cold-blooded killer. I understand, in a way. You need to be completely ruthless to get anything done. Risk death boldly, or starve like a coward.

The man patted the girl on the shoulder. —Are you feeling better?

She nodded and clutched her schoolbag tighter. —Right at the next junction.

—Right? Aren't you going to Yanfen Street?

—I want to go around the back.

I spun the wheel and pulled over to the side of the road. —Sorry, I can't hold it in any longer. If you aren't fussy, anywhere can be a toilet. Could you and the girl wait in the car for a minute?

The man frowned. —Turn left, it's just up ahead.

—Your daughter said turn right a moment ago. Make up your minds, I'm about to piss my pants.

—We're almost there.

I looked at him, sliding my hand smoothly into my jacket. —It's completely dark over there—are you sure there's a clinic?

The girl's eyes opened abruptly, her pupils huge. —Dad, I just farted, and now I feel better.

The man's jaw was set. —Better?

—Yes, I farted quietly, it didn't stink. I'm better now.

The man glanced at me. —I need a piss too. Wait in the car.

He got out, and so did I, taking the keys and locking the door behind me. The snow was falling heavily by this time, and the wind was strong, sliding down our collars into our clothes. The shantytown was only dimly visible, like a distant mountain range seen from a train. While the man slowly made his way down the bank to a thicket of grass and had a pee, I drew my gun and pointed it at his back. He turned around, still fastening his trousers.

—Hey, you've got the wrong idea.

—Stop what you're doing, and drop your pants.

—Ask around the factory, they'll tell you that I'm a good person.

—Shut up, pants off.

He let them fall to his ankles, and I got the cuffs from my belt.

—Don't let the child see—what will she think?

I aimed a kick at his underwear, and he didn't even try to dodge it.

—The clinic's just up ahead, it's a friend of mine's. You'll see for yourself.

That's when a truck hauling sand came barreling around the corner, and I suddenly realized I hadn't hit the hazard lights. The road was slick with snow. The truck seemed to hesitate for a moment, then collided with the taxi, sending it rolling down the slope toward us. A piece of glass the size of my palm sliced right into my head, and at the same instant, I fired my gun in the man's direction.

LI FEI

I don't know when it started, but my memories have become unbelievably clear—though I'm not sure how many of them actually happened and how many my brain just cobbled together from fragments of recollection.

Father often gets startled by what I remember from childhood. Occasionally I bring up something he's forgotten, every detail accurate, more than I should have been able to retain given my age at the time. But then he'll be chatting about something from just the week before, and I'll have forgotten it so completely, he'll wonder if it even happened at all.

I have no recollection of my mother's death, of course. I've seen pictures of her, but she just seemed like an unfamiliar woman. What turned her into a stranger? No particular reason, my father says, it's just that a woman always risks her life by giving birth, like a normal pedestrian hit by a drunk driver.

My father never remarried. At day care, the auntie wiped my butt and trained me to go to the toilet at particular times. If I pooped when I felt like it or got into a fight with another kid, she'd hit me. If I cried, a smack. If I kept crying, another smack, and let's see if you dare cry again. Of course, if I'd had a mother, she'd have done the same. This comforted me, that it was no big deal. Every evening, when the other kids were picked up by their mothers, I'd feel sorry for them, knowing

they faced more of the same treatment at home. Shame I didn't
get to hang on to that illusion for long.

Shu and his family lived in the middle of our row of
houses; we had the easternmost one. Every day, when my dad
got off work at the factory and came to get me, he'd wheel his
bicycle past their place. My father was a skillful bench worker.
The people who'd started at the plant the same time as him
were still called Young Zhao, Young Wang, Young Gao, while
my dad was Master Li. When my dad pushed me through
the factory, people would call out, Are you off, Master Li?
Going home to make dinner, Master Li? Got enough coal for
the winter, Master Li? Sometimes they came over to tease me
and try to get me to talk. My dad would smile and answer
briefly, but he hardly ever stopped to chat. They knitted him
scarves and sweaters, red, navy, dark blue, which he kept in
the closet with a bag of mothballs. I heard that he used to be
a difficult character when he was younger, but he mellowed
after marriage. He'd rather be taken advantage of than get into
arguments and cause unpleasantness. When my mother died,
he lost a bunch of weight, then learned to cook and gained it
back again. After getting promoted to factory supervisor, he
took on two apprentices. He didn't make them pour him tea
or wash his uniforms, just taught them everything he knew.
He could single-handedly assemble an entire engine with three
wrenches in two minutes and forty-five seconds. If I caught
him watching me at the nursery instead of playing cards after
lunch, that meant he was unhappy with his apprentices' work.

When I was six, I spoke to Shu for the first time, though
we'd seen each other around. I was a year older than him,
already in kindergarten. In the new year, I'd be starting elementary school. Shu was still in nursery, and was known in

the neighborhood for making mischief. One time, the kids were throwing a ball around when Shu kicked it into the ceiling light. Quite a few kids ended up with glass shards in their hair. The aunties didn't hit him; they just went to the distribution department to fetch his dad. Zhuang Dezeng sized up the situation, spoke to the aunties for a while, combed through the hair of the frightened kids, then went out to get two new fluorescent tubes and a big bag of White Rabbit sweets. He stood on a chair to install the new lights. The aunties held the chair steady, then helped him down to sit and eat melon seeds, laughing and chatting, before sending him on his way.

Shu's dad was full of life and had any number of skills. He was always nicely dressed and seemed able to accomplish things other people couldn't.

One summer evening, I traded my ice pop for the matches in Shu's hand.

For many nights afterward, I recalled that summer evening. To start with, I wanted to remember, and then it became a habit. This kept the memory from changing or disappearing into the darkness, like so many others.

I liked matches and was always stealing my dad's to play with. I set anything I could on fire. Normally, I was a well-behaved child who didn't talk too much, and when the aunties wouldn't let us use the toilet, I held it in. But I loved fire. Matches made me stare, transfixed. I burned my mother's letters to my dad, and that was one of a handful of times he actually hit me. After that, there were no more matches in our house. When I grabbed Shu's, I turned the matchbox into a fireball. I'd been holding in the urge for so long, I didn't even care that I'd scorched the skin off my fingers. The fireball fell to earth and went out. I burst into tears, not out of fear but, rather, because of the game's extravagance.

My dad was furious, but he couldn't bear to hit me. —Look at this child, Auntie Fu, just look at this child.

Fu Dongxin said: —You like matches?

I plucked at the skin on my hand and didn't say anything.

—Why?

I was silent.

My dad tapped my shoulder. —Hey, Auntie Fu's talking to you.

—They're pretty.

—Pretty how?

—The flames.

—Come here.

She grabbed my hand and inspected it. —This girl may accomplish great things in the future.

—Like what?

—I don't know, but she's curious. Shu's too young, he won't sit still. Whatever I teach him, he forgets immediately.

—He's four, let him play.

—If you trust me, send her over after dinner or during the day on weekends. I have lots of books here, and I too played with fire as a kid.

—Oh no, I couldn't put you and Dezeng to so much trouble.

Zhuang Dezeng said: —What trouble? Now that we can only have one child, these kids could keep each other company. Dongxin has a bellyful of learning—you think she can talk to me about that?

My dad turned to me. —Quick, thank Auntie and Uncle.

I did as I was told. All this while, Shu had been sitting on the ground studying the popsicle stick, which was crawling with ants, most of whom had gotten stuck and couldn't pull themselves free.

The next day was a school day, and I couldn't wait for evening to come—but when it did, my dad just made dinner as usual and set up the little table on the heated kang. We ate sitting across from each other, not talking much. He said nothing about this new plan. I went to bed and sobbed with disappointment under the covers, scraping bits of plaster off the walls and chewing on them until I fell asleep. Then it was Sunday. I woke up to find my dad out and the door locked. He usually locked me in like this when he had stuff to do on Sunday. I didn't bother drawing the curtains, just washed my face and brushed my teeth, then went to find something to eat on the stove. My dad came back covered in sweat, bearing half a rack of ribs, two bags of Nation's Glory apples, and a box of Autumn Forest snacks. He got me to change into clean clothes and pulled the curtains open. The outside world was dazzling. He put on his faded work uniform and newly issued green rubber shoes. Then he picked up the goods, took my hand, and brought me to Shu's house.

Shu's dad was polishing his leather shoes, and Shu was blowing soap bubbles. Fu Dongxin sat on the kang, drawing on a sheet of paper. Shu's dad looked up and said, Oh, you're here. My dad said, Is this a good time? Then he went into the house, put the gifts on the side table, and told me, Say hello to Teacher Fu.

FU DONGXIN

On July 12, 1995, Shu got into a fight. He led a gang to a neighboring school, where they broke an eleventh grader's

nose and left him with a mild concussion. It happened late in
the day, and I only found out the following morning, just as
I was giving Li Fei her lesson. We were talking about Exodus
in the Old Testament, where Jehovah says to Moses, *Wherefore
criest thou unto me? Speak unto the children of Israel, that they
go forward. But lift thou up thy rod, and stretch out thine hand
over the sea, and divide it: and the children of Israel shall go on
dry ground through the midst of the sea.* Shu's teacher came into
our courtyard and told me what had happened. Shu wasn't
home—he'd taken his ball and gone out earlier. I told Li Fei to
continue reading the story—even if she didn't believe it, she
still could appreciate the energy in the words. If Shu comes
home, I said, tell him to stay here until I get back. Then I collected my savings book and went to the bank to withdraw fifteen hundred yuan. I tried to give two hundred to the teacher,
but he refused. Shu's father, Dezeng, took good care of him
every New Year, he said, and anyway it's normal for boys to
get into trouble, but Shu shouldn't get involved in gang fights.
Half-grown kids don't know their own strength—what if they
caused a tragedy? And if he dared to attack an eleventh grader,
what might he do next? The teacher brought me to visit the
victim, who'd just been discharged from the hospital. I gave
him a bag of fruit, stuffed the money into his parents' hands,
and sat down for a chat. The couple sold silk scarves at Wu
Ai Market and did quite well for themselves. We managed to
come to an agreement. As they saw me off, they said, Look at
you, all civilized, how come your son's so delinquent? I didn't
say anything, just took the bus home.

Back at the house, Shu was pestering Li Fei to play ball
with him. He placed two rocks in the courtyard, cajoled her
to stand between them to serve as the goalkeeper, and kicked

the ball right into her face. She reeled from the impact, ran to fetch the ball, and tossed it back to him.

I yelled at Shu: —Get into the house right now!

He kicked the ball to Li Fei. —Go on, practice, don't play like a retard.

She grabbed the ball and followed him into the house. I sat on the stool and made him stand. —I've called your dad; he's coming back tomorrow.

—You're just trying to frighten me, Mom. Dad's only been gone a few days—I know he won't be back so soon.

—Stand up straight. What did you say to Li Fei just now?

—Nothing. Can't I call a stupid person stupid?

—Say sorry to her right now.

Li Fei was still clutching the ball. —Teacher Fu, he didn't do it on purpose, and anyway I really am stupid.

—See? She agrees.

—Apologize.

—But you told me we have to be true to ourselves, and if I said sorry I wouldn't mean it.

—I want you to apologize for real.

—I can't do that.

Li Fei said: —Shu, do you want to play ball?

He didn't even look at her. —No, I'm never playing with you again.

I said: —Fei, you've been hanging out with him since you were small, and you're older than him—haven't you played enough?

Li Fei didn't respond.

—Zhuang Shu, when your dad gets back tomorrow, I'll have him speak to you. I know you won't listen to me.

An hour before this, I'd gone to the public phone and

called Dezeng to tell him Shu was in trouble again, and this time it was gang violence, a mob of them against one kid. Dezeng got worked up.

—I'll come back from Yunnan tomorrow.

—Have you done everything you needed to do?

—Our relationships here are solid now, and they were very happy with the packaging samples I brought.

—They really found them acceptable?

—They'd never seen such fine drawings.

—Then strike while the iron's hot; I'll talk to our child.

—Talking won't work. I'll have to come back anyway—I have a meeting at the Shenyang tobacco plant. Everyone's contracting stuff out these days, so I want to talk to them about taking over the factory's printing press and running it privately. We're going to have our own business.

When Shu saw that I wasn't bluffing, he got flustered. —The other kid hit me first, him and his friends, and that's why I hit him back.

I felt my hands trembling. —Did you know hitting people is a sin?

—What?

—It doesn't matter what your reasons are, hitting people is a sin. Did you know that?

—So other people can hit me, but I can't hit them back? Anyone can just take a swing at me?

I looked at him, that round face just like Dezeng's, the short, stubborn hair. Three of us in this family, and the pair of them looked so alike.

I clasped my hands to stop the shaking. —Never mind that, let's talk about what you called Fei. Why can't you respect other people?

He turned to Li Fei. —Big Sister Fei, maybe I shouldn't
have done that.

—You call that an apology? You know Fei is a shy girl, so
you ought to protect her, but instead you bully her—what
kind of animal are you? If this were the Cultural Revolution, I
suppose you'd have turned on your mother, too?

—What's the Cultural Revolution?

—Never mind, just make a proper apology.

He turned to Li Fei. —Big Sister Fei, I shouldn't have done
that, I didn't mean to. Next time I'll stand in the goal and you
can kick the ball at me, and when we're grown up, if anyone
treats you badly, I'll make sure he dies.

I said: —That's the right idea, but you might want to improve
the wording.

Li Fei said: —I'll remember that.

—Go play in the courtyard, Shu; Fei and I are going to
continue our lesson.

I got Li Fei to sit on the kang and read Exodus out loud.
Then I explained a few points I thought she'd be able to
grasp.

—Fei, how long have you been studying with me?

—Six or seven years.

—Do you find this meaningful?

—Yes, I wish it were evening all day long.

—The first time I saw you, I knew you were a good seed-
ling, and sure enough, I was right—the progress you've made,
you know more than most senior high students now.

—I'm not sure about that.

—No matter what, you have to read and write the way you
want to. Read more, write more.

—Okay.

—You'll be taking the entrance exam soon—make sure you get into senior high.

—Even if I get in, it costs nine thousand yuan, so I'm not going, though my father wants me to.

—Tell your father to come and see me; I'll give you the cash. I know he's out of work and money's tight, but you can pay us back when things are better. It's a good time for you—back when I wanted to study, there was nowhere I could go. Remember, as long as you have knowledge and a skill, there's nothing to fear.

—I can't take your money.

—You should. I won't be able to teach you much longer.

She looked up. —Why?

—They're going to tear down these houses, and we'll all have to move. We won't be neighbors for much longer. You know why I taught you Exodus today?

—I won't see Shu anymore?

—I picked this book because I wanted you to know that as long as what's in your heart is genuine and sincere, the mountains and oceans will part for you, and the people coming after you, the ones who didn't make space for you, will all get punished. When you're grown, when you're older, I want you to hold on to that thought.

Li Fei didn't say anything, just looked out the window. I wasn't sure if she'd understood what I was trying to tell her.

LI FEI

The Sundays of my memory were always sunny. My father would open all the windows, set a basin of water on the edge of the kang, and wipe every pane of glass clean. Then he'd pour the dirty water out in the courtyard and start on the bedding. Both hands working away, he'd wring the sheets section by section and hang them on the washing line, so the courtyard filled with the fragrance of soap. He'd sit down for a cigarette, then clean the stovetop and floors, his muscular arms going like a pair of oars, rowing to every corner of our house. The final chore would be winding our wall clock. He'd open the red cover, produce a gleaming key, and turn it so it went *click-clack*. On tiptoe and craning his neck, as if to see something through the clockface.

The factory seemed to collapse all at once, but actually there'd been warning signs for some time. For a while, the TV kept telling us the country was struggling under a heavy burden and every regular person had to play a part in lightening the load, as if the nation were a poor little widow. My father continued showing up for work at the usual time, but sometimes he didn't change into a clean uniform at the end of the day, because there'd been nothing for him to do, and he hadn't sweated.

The day he learned that he'd been laid off, I was at home lighting the stove. I loved to watch the flames rise up from below, squirming their way into the belly of the stove, like a heart birthing itself in the palm of my hand. I didn't even notice my dad when he walked in. The smoke had got into my eyes, and only when I wiped away my tears did I realize he was squatting next to me, tossing matches onto the fire. His jaw was swollen at a funny angle, and he had a black eye.

—Dad, what happened?

—It's nothing, I fell off my bike. Let's have dumplings tonight.

He put his face under the faucet to wash the blood off his mouth, then set a big pot of water boiling and started wrapping dumplings. His hands were big and coarse, but his actions were deft: *tok tok tok*, chopping up the filling, dropping a portion onto the dough, and pinching it shut.

As we ate our dinner, he had some sorghum spirits. My dad seldom drank, and the bottle of Old Dragon Mouth had a layer of dust on it when he got it from the cupboard. The drink was almost gone when he said:

—I've been laid off.

—Oh. Why?

—Almost everyone was let go. The factory can't go on. It's fine, I'll think of something, you just get on with your studies.

—So you didn't fall down today.

—I didn't.

—What happened?

—I was wondering what I could do. I thought maybe I could sell tea eggs; I've seen people doing brisk business at the square. After work, I went there to watch. I was about to leave when a bunch of people showed up in uniform and kicked over their stoves. One woman held on to hers and wouldn't let go, so an officer grabbed her by the hair and started dragging her to his car. I walked over and grabbed ahold of him.

—Dad!

—There were too many of them; I'd have been fine if I were still young.

He spread open his right hand and looked at it. —I couldn't take them.

—Did you think about me?

—I came home to get a knife, but I saw you lighting the stove, and I was scared to die.

—I'm not taking the entrance exam; I'll just go wherever they send me.

He stood up. —Get on with your studies—don't make me say it again.

He finished his drink, put away the crockery, and didn't say another word for the rest of the night.

ZHUANG DEZENG

One summer, I can't remember exactly which year—those years passed in a flash, blurring together—but probably around the millennium, I was on a business trip in Beijing when I got a phone call: —Foreman Zhuang, they're tearing down the Chairman. Can you stop them?

It was a retired worker, one of those I'd taken over along with the printing press.

—Which Chairman?

—The six-meter-tall one in Red Flag Square—he'll be gone the day after tomorrow.

I knew the one he meant; it was near where I'd lived as a child. His fleshy jowls spread in a smile, one arm outstretched as if reaching for something. In the summer and fall, we flew kites around there, and in the winter we'd crowd around him, spinning tops on the ice.

—Why are they doing that?

—To replace him with a bird.

—A bird?

—Something called a sunbird, a big yellow statue. I heard it was designed by some foreigner. It's two meters taller than the Chairman.

—I'm not the city council secretary, I can't do anything about this. The Chairman's dead, just let him go. Don't bother yourselves about this—it's not like it will affect your pension.

With that, I hung up.

The next evening, I got back to Shenyang and had to go straight to another business engagement. It went on so long that when we finally went to the bathhouse to relax, I fell asleep. By the time I woke up, it was noon and the others had left, sticking me with the tab. I phoned my driver to pick me up, and halfway home, I had to get out to vomit. Last night's liquor had burned a passage through my gut. A group of old people in work uniforms were walking down the middle of the road in somewhat ragged formation, absolutely silent. The driver said, What's going on? Some sort of fitness campaign? I had no idea either, so I waved his question away and slumped over in the back seat. When we got to my front door, I suddenly realized: the Chairman. They were on their way to the Chairman. I dismissed the driver and sat on the curb for a while. I looked down at my trousers: spotless. And my leather shoes: also spotless. What a change. A few years ago, as I wandered the plains of Yunnan, my shoes would split open after just a few days, and my trousers were permanently caked in yellow dirt. I glanced at my watch. At this hour, Zhuang Shu would be at school, and Dongxin was probably taking an afternoon nap. Ever since she'd quit her job, her naps had grown longer and longer, as if sleep were her main task of the day. I stood up, hailed a taxi, and directed the driver to Red Flag Square.

On the other side of the protective screen, the driver was in his uniform, which included a gray cap. The strange thing was, he wore a face mask too, even though it was a stifling afternoon in August and he must have been sweltering. I glanced at him in the rearview mirror and met his gaze: he'd been staring at me. One of his eyes drooped down at the corner. I quickly looked away.

—Red Flag Square?

—Yes.

He turned off the "For Hire" sign. We hadn't gone far when the Chairman's huge, unsupported arm became visible, but the traffic suddenly slowed to a standstill. Apparently, the old people I'd seen earlier were just one of many contingents. As I watched, another platoon marched slowly down the middle of the road, this group wearing a different color and style of uniform. The driver rested one arm on the open window and stared at them, not honking his horn, not doing anything at all, just calmly watching. I said:

—What a waste of time.

—Huh?

I pointed ahead of us.

—So why are you going?

I hadn't expected him to talk back. —I have business nearby, nothing to do with the Chairman statue.

He nodded. —Doing business? Dressed like that?

—Do I know you?

—No, why?

—You're being very rude. Do we know each other from somewhere?

—You're a fine gentleman, and I actually work for a living—don't give me too much credit.

I had nothing to say to that. Maybe I'd drunk too much the night before and my brain wasn't working right.

Finally, we reached the traffic island around the square.

—Where to?

I glanced at the square. —Around the island.

—Can't you see it's completely jammed?

—Just drive. If you think it's taking too long, I'll pay you double.

—Fine by me. People like you must have money to burn.

—What's your problem?

—I'm a taxi driver, not your slave. Get out of my car.

I glanced at his scarred face in the rearview mirror, but he didn't meet my eye. Resentful people tend to be loudmouths, or else they're stubborn as mules. Leaving and hailing another taxi wouldn't get me anywhere—more and more old people kept pouring through the spaces between vehicles, surging like water toward the square. I said: —Listen, it's such a hot day, let's calm down. Drive around once, and then we can go back the way we came.

He didn't say anything, just turned toward the inner ring of the circle. Through the window, hordes of people sat around the Chairman. The cranes and forklifts of the demolition crew were parked in one corner, and several police officers stood around with loudspeakers, not shouting but drinking water. The old people sat in the hot sun, their white hair giving off a frosty gleam. One of them, maybe about seventy, stood beneath the Chairman's sleeve and led them in a song with a small wooden baton. On his right, another old man sat on a folding stool, pulling on an accordion, a rolled cigarette hanging off his lips. He kept flicking it up to take another drag.

> Beijing's gold mountain blazes with light,
> Our Chairman Mao is glorious and bright,
> Much kindness and warmth he sends our way,

To liberated peasants he brings delight.
Let us all march toward socialism. Hey!

Ropes hung from the Chairman's neck, swaying in the wind. Several workers sat in the shade behind him, chatting away, as if this scene didn't concern them. Once these old farts were done complaining, all the workers had to do was extend a finger to send the Chairman tumbling down. I remembered how, as a child, I'd stood with a few other kids in the same place, looking at the back of the Chairman's head. One of us said, Do you think his head really is that big? Someone responded, Nonsense, that would make him a monster. My big brother immediately smacked him and said, Have you ever seen the goddamn Chairman? Shut your big fat mouth. I briefly wondered whether the Chairman's head really was enormous—how many of our army caps could his be made into? But no, when he'd inspected the Red Guards, his head had looked to be about the same size as theirs, so surely it must be normal. Someone from our school had joined the Red Guards, and his head was no bigger than mine.

Traffic crept slowly forward. The drivers and their passengers, whether they were in private cars, trucks, or taxis, all had more than enough time to gawk at the square and the old people in it. I hadn't been here in a very long time—hardly at all, since I'd moved away. This statue was like a big old tree anchoring my hometown. I once got shat on by the birds that nested on the statue. So many evenings watching the sun set here, when I was young and had nothing better to do. Over the last few years, I'd completely forgotten that time, as if it never happened at all, as if I'd appeared fully formed as my present self.

—You know how many there are?

—What?

We were almost all the way around the circle. I was starting to get the impression that the driver was going even slower than the other vehicles.

—Never mind. Where to next?

I looked at the square, which was motionless as a picture.

—Back the way we came.

He shifted gears. —Why do you think they're protesting there?

—Nostalgia, I guess.

—No, they're upset. They wonder, if Chairman Mao were still alive, would the Party behave like this?

—So they're just venting their frustration.

—They remind me of dolphins.

—What?

—I saw it on the news. When the sea gets polluted, dolphins crawl up onto the beach to kill themselves. A whole row of them, all lined up, dead.

I didn't say anything.

—Cowards, all of them. Dolphins have teeth, couldn't they fight back? So what if these people are over seventy? They can still hold a knife. You can't be sure your life was worth it until the day you die. Don't you think?

—Not really—as long as you're alive, there's hope.

—Hope isn't evenly distributed. People like you hoard it all.

Now I was sure he knew me. If only I could rip off his mask. Instead, I sat in the back seat of that taxi and tried to remember. His voice. His posture. Familiar, and yet not. Things kept getting in the way and obstructing my memory.

When we got to our destination, he flicked the "For Hire" sign on and said:

—Twenty-nine yuan. You know how many there are?

I took out my wallet. —How many what?

—Soldiers guarding the Chairman—how many do you think there are?

—I counted them just now, but I really can't remember.

He took the money in silence, waited for me to open the door and leave, then stuck his head out the window and said:

—Thirty-six. Twenty-eight men, eight women, five with armbands, nine with army caps, seven in helmets, three with machine guns, two with bayonets.

He stepped on the gas and sped off.

ZHUANG SHU

After I'd rejected my dad's wishes by becoming a police officer, he stopped helping me out. While my mother was on vacation in England, he and I made an agreement that for the first five years of my working life, I wasn't allowed to ask him for money. To be honest, I'd already made this decision for myself, only without the five-year limit. My relationship with my parents was unusual. I'd never been close to my mother, not since I was a child. I didn't care about book learning, so she devoted herself to teaching this other kid, a girl from down the street, passing on the contents of her treasure trove. When the girl was twelve, we moved and lost touch with her. I once snuck a look at my mother's diary and found out that over the years, she'd spent quite a lot of energy tracking down her former student but wasn't able to find a single clue, as if this person had never existed, as if someone had waved a hand and erased all those months and years they spent together, huddled on the kang reading. Later on, she got into foreign vacations, and our house filled with paintings, porcelain, and souvenirs from her travels. My dad cleared out a large room for her to store her finds in. Exorbitant, unique artworks sat cheek by jowl with cheap, mass-produced tourist gewgaws. My father had first established himself by printing cigarette packets, and there was a time when, due to his monopoly, his presses might as well have been printing money. Later, he got into real estate, restaurants, car accessories, and baby-care products. In my third year of college, I took a girl to see a movie, and just as we started kissing, I saw his name out the corner of my eye—he was one of the producers. His whole life was squeaky clean. He did everything my mother asked of him, and as soon as he got into the cigarette-packet game, he quit smoking himself. He seldom mentioned his business allies and rivals, and I feel like in his heart of hearts, he saw these people as the same: they needed each other, and they exhausted each other. My impression is that even when he got completely smashed, he would always find his way home. My mother never complained, just made him a bowl of noodles, or on the occasions when he collapsed as soon as he stepped inside, she'd drag him to bed and shut the door. My father often said I was rebellious and we had nothing in common, but actually I embodied every quality of our family: stubborn, earnest, ascetic, long-memoried. The older I got, the more like them I became; they just didn't recognize it.

I got into a fight one time in senior high, and as the ring-leader, I was locked up all night at the jailhouse while the others were sent home. I had a small cut on my brow, so the volunteer officer on duty brought me a bandage and passed it through the bars. I remember he was very young—my facial hair was thicker than his.

—You know what happens to gangsters?

Silence. I stuck the bandage crosswise over my eyebrow.

—Either they become habitual offenders, or they become even more ordinary than ordinary people.

Silence.

—You think you're so cool? What do you think you'll ever accomplish?

Silence.

He sat with one foot resting on the other knee and flicked his lighter. —You know how many police officers die every day in this country?

Silence.

—I've looked at your case file. You're in and out of here all the time, always because you decided to stand up for someone else. What do you think is going to happen to you? When those friends of yours walked out of here, did any of them so much as glance back?

—Listen, motherfucker, come in here and fight me if you have the balls.

—Fight? I could kill you with a single bullet, and that would be legal—do you even know how to hold a gun? Fucking idiot.

I reached through the bars and grabbed his uniform. He didn't resist.

—Have a good feel, this is a police uniform. A drug dealer here yesterday hacked his own parents to death so he could steal six hundred yuan. Before the father died, he told his son where the money was hidden and said to run as fast as he

could. Would you dare go after someone like that, you jerk?
You're all just a bunch of morons.

With that, he wrenched my hand away and walked off,
not looking back. I heard his footsteps fade as he walked out
the door.

I've always remembered that man, down to his badge number. He was an unregistered auxiliary officer who, I would discover, didn't even have the right to use a gun. A couple of years
later, one of my friends was taken in on charges of assault. I
got some money from my dad and went to help him. I was
nineteen at the time, repeating the fourth year of senior high.
Quite a few officers recognized me, and one of them said, You
haven't been here for a while. Did you go into business with
your dad?

I said no, then asked after the auxiliary officer, described
him and gave his badge number, and asked if he was still there.
I don't know why I wanted to see him, but I'd never forgotten
him, and quite a few times he'd come to mind when I was
challenged to a fight.

—Why do you want to see him?

—No reason, just asking.

—Someone took revenge.

I stared at him, waiting for him to say more.

—He died in the lobby of his apartment building. Stabbed
from behind. He was about to get married, too—the wedding
banquet had been arranged.

I wanted to ask if they'd caught the murderer, but no sound
came from my throat, as if something was stuck there. I dealt
with the paperwork, but when my friend walked over smiling,
I found I had nothing to say, so I just turned and walked away.

From the time I got accepted to the police academy to

when I graduated, my mom didn't speak much to me, but before I took the entrance test, she suddenly asked, Are you really going to be a police officer?

—Yes.

—Why?

It was morning, and we were both at the breakfast table. She took a sip of milk and gently wiped the white froth from her mouth.

—Everyone dies sooner or later, right?

—Indeed.

—In my time on earth, I want a job that means something. To others as well as to me. There aren't many of those.

—If you say so.

She looked down and drank her milk in silence. Later, my dad told me she'd said to him that if I didn't get in, he should pull some strings and make sure I had a place. I don't know what was going on in her head. Maybe the way she saw it, it didn't matter what I did, since I wouldn't ever be the sort of person she'd hoped for anyway. Throughout my four years in the academy, she didn't come to visit once, not even for my graduation. For the first time in my life, I was top of the class, and still she didn't appear. Instead it was my dad who drove to the school and attended the ceremony. He even bought me dinner afterward, at a Western restaurant. He said my mom was in South Africa and he couldn't get hold of her, but she'd sent a gift: a drawing of a little boy standing between two rocks, guarding the goal, while a girl pulled her leg back, ready to send the ball flying toward him. A simple rendering, pencil on regular A4 paper, no signature, no date.

During the meal, my dad tried to persuade me to get a desk job in the municipal department. When I refused, he called for the check before we'd finished eating, and walked out of the restaurant.

Sometime after making my deal with him, I waited till my parents were out to grab my stuff and move into a work dormitory. I'd successfully applied for a position as a probationary criminal police officer. In the first six months, I took part in several easy operations, going after suspects on the run. Together with a bunch of older cops, I went to seven or eight provincial towns—villages, workplaces, coal mines—to bring back criminals who'd evaded justice for years or even decades. They weren't dangerous. I remember one guy who had just come up from the mine. When he saw us, he said, I'll just have a shower. One of the old cops said, There's no time, the car's waiting. With that, he walked over and cuffed the criminal. His hair was covered in coal dust; any one of my childhood playmates would have looked tougher than this guy. He said, Can I go home to see my wife and daughter? The old cop said, Get them to come visit you. On the road to the airport, he said, If only you'd come sooner—I've ruined things for those two.

In September 2007, I became a full-fledged police officer. Now I could request a gun while on patrol or, if it was an important case, wear one at all times. On the evening of September 4, a city official from the Heping District Law Enforcement Brigade got drunk and, on his way home, took a shortcut through a park, where he was shot and dumped in the artificial lake. The city's Criminal Division held a meeting, and the core cadres met separately to analyze the case. This was the second member of the force to be attacked that month. The first had been struck on the back of the head with a blunt object, collapsed at his building entrance, and never got up again. Because I'd graduated with decent results, I was allowed to listen in on these meetings. The weapon in this new case was a Type 64 7.62mm police revolver, and the bullet was police-issued too. The victim had also been hit from behind with a blunt instrument, probably a hammer or wrench, but the pathologist indicated that this wasn't the cause of death. Though injured, he'd tried to run, and that's when the attacker shot him. I didn't know this official—we were in different departments—but I attended his funeral anyway. The higher-ups had insisted on a simple ceremony. In his portrait, the deceased wore civvies rather than a uniform, and looked quite relaxed. The serial number of the revolver was tracked to a cop named Jiang Bufan who, twelve years ago, had been left in a coma after an unsuccessful sting operation in which the killer got away—not sure if this was lucky or unlucky for the officer; his head was split by flying glass from a car window, then bashed in. Because this was a workplace injury, all his medical expenses were covered by the city. Although thirty-seven, he was still a bachelor at the time, so his parents took care of him right up until his death three years later. He never woke up, never uttered another word. Another consequence of this incident was that both of his Type 64 revolvers went missing, along with two magazines containing a total of four teen bullets.

The case in question was a series of taxi driver murders. It was never solved, but after Jiang Bufan's injury, the killings stopped. As for the two murdered city officials, they were both notorious. A month before, while clearing the street of illegal vendors, they'd confiscated a woman's corn-roasting pot. During the struggle, the woman's twelve-year-old daughter fell onto the stove, sustaining serious burns—she'd probably be scarred for life. Pictures of the two officials were splashed across various newspapers and news sites, but the official verdict was that the girl had slipped and fallen, and her mother was held responsible. The two officials got away with a warning—a slap on the wrist—and kept their jobs.

At the second case-analysis meeting, the room was wreathed in cigarette smoke. The chief in charge of the investigation, Mo Xiaodong, had been a part of the manhunt that went wrong all those years ago. His wife had been heavily pregnant at the time, and now he was the father of a twelve-year-old son, while his old buddy Jiang Bufan had been dead for almost a decade, leaving no offspring. Jiang's father was dead too, and only his old mother was still alive. Mo visited several times a year, always bringing a gift, whatever he could spare. He intended to go on investigating this case, he said, past retirement if necessary. If he died without cracking it, he'd make his son become an officer to carry on the work. The room was absolutely silent, and I bet most people were thinking two things: first, how this case was so much more difficult because there weren't as many security cameras around back then, and second, how many bullets were left in those two guns.

For the first time since I'd started sitting in on these meetings, I spoke: —Sirs, I'm new here, but I just want to say a few words, please correct me if I'm wrong.

Commander Mo said: —No need to be so polite.

—I've looked at the archive files and the photos of the crime scene, and went there myself.

—When?

—Yesterday, after the funeral. I took a bus there.

—Who told you to go?

—No one, I just wanted to see it for myself.

—Carry on.

—It used to be a sorghum plantation, but now it's all built up, selling at two hundred yuan per square foot, and the dirt road is now a four-lane tarmac. The field where Jiang Bufan was found is now a Walmart—the landscape from the photos is nowhere to be seen.

—Are you planning to go into fucking real estate?

—I'm getting to the point. I looked at newspapers from the time and asked the locals, and I discovered something: heading east from the scene, not far away, there's a private traditional Chinese clinic. It was there twelve years ago, and it's still there now. I hung around the entrance until an older patient came out. He said the doctor here used to be Sun Yuxin, a worker who'd studied medicine with a traditional healer in the village he was sent down to during the Cultural Revolution. He set up a clinic the year after he lost his job, and managed to keep it going until he died of pancreatic cancer last spring. Now the clinic is run by his son, Sun Tianbo.

Everyone was staring at me. Commander Mo tapped his cigarette on the ashtray. —Continue.

—This case resulted in one death and one injury: Jiang Bufan eventually died, and the truck driver Liu Lei banged his head on the steering wheel and fainted from loss of blood. All he remembers is a red car suddenly appearing in front of him. He was exhausted at the time of the crash and claims it all went black. I wouldn't count him as a witness. There were traces of blood in the back of the taxi that didn't belong to Jiang Bufan. Supposedly these came from the murderer, but Jiang was outside the car when he was hit by flying glass. My theory is that apart from Jiang and the killer, there was a third person in the taxi.

—What's your name?

—Zhuang Shu.

—Nice work, Officer Zhuang. Go talk to the family. Now keep talking.

—This person remained in the car after Jiang Bufan and the killer got out, probably in the passenger seat, and was seriously wounded when the truck hit the taxi and it overturned. Jiang Bufan was out cold, so the killer took his guns, rescued this third person from the vehicle, and fled the scene. This explains why the weapon that Jiang had hidden in the car disappeared, too. If he hadn't had to go back for someone, how would the murderer have found the gun?

Commander Mo stood up. —You mean they went to that clinic?

—That's just a hunch—I didn't go in because I didn't want to show our hand, but I believe it's a possibility.

SUN TIANBO

I saw my father twice after his death. The first time, I was in the city library borrowing some books for my dear friend Fei. I had the most expensive membership, which allowed me to take out ten books at a time. I knew this library well. It was newly constructed and had a lawn outside, which made it look attractive from a distance. A long flight of stone steps led up to the entrance, and every visitor had to ascend as if they were paying their respects at a mountain monastery. Sitting in the reading room, if night happened to fall before closing time, you'd see a broad street far below, where countless dimly visible vehicles crawled by beneath the streetlamps. The interior was fairly spartan. All the literature and history books were on the first floor, less than a thousand square meters in all. The second floor had multimedia reading rooms, though I don't know their holdings because Fei never needed any books from upstairs. Every time she asked for books, I closed the clinic for the day. I'd arrive at the library in the morning, get the ones she wanted, sit in the reading room, and go through all the forewords and afterwords. If they seemed interesting, I'd start at the beginning and read a few dozen pages. When the attendants in their white gloves came by to reshelve the books others had left on the tables and chairs, I knew it was time for me to leave. That day, the ten books I borrowed were: *The Pentateuch*; Shuntarō Tanikawa's *The Day the Birds Disappeared from the Sky*; *West with the Night*; *Speak, Memory*; *The Ballad of the Sad Café*; *Hard-Boiled Wonderland and the End of the World*; *The Problems of Philosophy*; *As I Lay Dying*; *The Big Sleep*; and *The Corrections*. I spent the afternoon getting through the first part of *The Problems of Philosophy*, which was mostly about a table. This writer went on and on, but it was all meaningless. "Is there any knowledge in the world which is so certain that no reasonable man could doubt it? This question, which at first sight might not seem difficult, is really one of the most difficult that can be asked." There seemed to be some kind of theory there but not much actual knowledge.

I left the library with the books in two plastic bags and was trying to get a taxi home when my father walked out of a nearby noodle shop.

—I'll help you carry one of those.

I could smell the garlic on his breath. He'd loved eating the stuff when he was still alive—he said it prevented cancer.

—I can manage.

—It's pinching your hand. Give it here.

I ignored him and opened the taxi door. He gestured for me to scoot in, then sat next to me in the back.

—You look pale, you must be working too hard. Let me take your pulse.

—I'm fine, I just slept late.

—Things haven't been right around here recently.

—I know.

—Shall I tell you about me and your Uncle Li?

—You've already told me.

—I'll tell you again.

—Fine.

—Not long after I was sent down, I joined the security team. Your Uncle Li was our leader. I knew him when we were kids—he and his brothers were known as the "Three Tigers." We were close, and though I was older, I was happy to run around with him. Whatever he said, I would do. He put me on gambling patrol. One time, we were closing in on a house when a player jumped out the window and tried to run. I reached out to catch him, and he stabbed me. Your Uncle Li carried me on his back to Old Mr. Ma, who used acupuncture to seal my veins and stop the bleeding. Li saved my life. Then he tracked down the guy and snapped the tendons in his legs.

—Yup, that's the same story.

—If he gets caught, Fei will be an orphan.

—I know what I'm doing.

—There's no need to rush things with you and Fei. She's a strange one, doesn't get out much, just keeps to herself and writes.

—I'm not planning to make a move anytime soon.

—I know this isn't easy for you, but sometimes that's how

things are in this world. I had to keep Old Li's secret after he told me everything that day, and now you must do the same for Li Fei.

—Stay out of this. Fei and I are just friends, like you and Uncle Li were.

—If you say so. Anyway, tell Fei to use the back door from now on, so no one sees her coming in. Or maybe tell her to stop visiting altogether.

—Stop worrying. You lived your whole life, it's time for you to rest.

He patted me on the hand and left.

The second time I saw him was after two police officers came by. That night, he nudged me awake. —Son, if you can't handle this, just get out. But make sure Fei is taken care of.

—You've changed your tune; you must be getting old.

Then I shut my eyes and went back to sleep.

FU DONGXIN

There was a night before we moved when Dezeng wasn't home, and I went to speak with Old Li, partly about the future—Fei's education—and partly about the past. When I reached his front door, I saw him on the kang fixing the wall clock. Fei wasn't there—she was at a school gathering. It was the autumn of 1995, and you could still see stars in the city sky. I stood in his courtyard watching him take that clock apart, hooking out each tiny component with a nail, wiping it, then tightening it back in place with a screwdriver. Above us was Orion with his belt, the arrogant bastard. The courtyard was piled high with old things: suitcases, a credenza, leather shoes, pots, ladles.

Items to be sold—Old Li and Fei couldn't bring everything with them when they moved. Maybe the clock would be sold too, after repairs. I knocked on the door. He looked up.

—Oh, it's you, Teacher Fu.

—I keep telling you not to call me that; that's what Fei calls me.

He clicked the last component neatly into place and climbed off the kang. —Please have a seat, Teacher Fu.

I sat. He washed his hands with soap and went out into the courtyard to fetch the tea leaves. I said:

—You sit too, I want to talk to you about Fei.

—I've been sitting for too long, I feel like standing.

—I saw Fei's results in the practice exams. She scored thirty points more than the best high school requirements.

—That's because you taught her well.

—I haven't taught her anything for the test—that was all her own work.

—The child knows how to apply herself.

—Don't worry about the fees, we have some money that's just sitting there.

—I'm not worried, I can provide for my own child, but thank you for the thought.

—In ancient times, after apprentices finished training and came down from the mountain, their masters would give them a sword or money for the journey. No need to be polite: if you won't accept a gift, then call it a loan, and you can pay me back later.

He picked up my cup from the kang table, tossed out the cooled liquid, and refreshed it with hot water.

—Here, this is warm. Cold tea is bad for your stomach. I had apprentices too, though I got fired after I'd finished training them. Now they're striking at the factory, and I'm sitting around at home. But I'm not ashamed; it's not as though we're begging.

I reached into my pocket for the envelope of cash, but he caught my arm.

—Don't, Teacher Fu. It's fine to make the offer, but if you take that out, I'll have to scold you.

I looked into his eyes, which were enormous and bright, not murky like most people who'd spent too much time at the factory. I let the envelope stay where it was.

—I understand. You're saying this is between you and Fei.

—Each of us has our own road to walk, and like I said, I appreciate the thought.

For a while, neither of us spoke. I looked at the exposed clockwork on the table, going *tick-tick* as it turned. I said:

—There was one more thing I wanted to ask you. I'm moving away tomorrow.

—Go on.

—Won't you sit down? I feel like I'm lecturing you.

On this September night, he was wearing a white shirt that exposed most of his arms, gnarled as tree branches, their contours plainly visible, a Seagull watch on his wrist. Although he'd just been hard at work, he looked clean and fresh, not sweaty at all. He fiddled with his watch strap, sitting diagonally across from me, his leg dangling in the air.

—Did you know about me before we met, Mr. Li?

—No, I only discovered how much learning you had after you moved here.

— But I knew you.

—Oh?

—In '68, my father was beaten up, and you saved him.

—Really? I don't remember. How is he now?

—His mind is going, and he's deaf in one ear, but otherwise he's in good health.

—That's lucky. One less thing to worry about.

He paused a moment. —That's how things were back then. I've beaten people too, you just didn't see it.

I lifted my cup to my lips and had a sip of tea—still warm.

—My dad had a coworker, a professor from the literature department, back from his studies in America. When I was little, they would get together to recite Walt Whitman's poetry and play records. During the Cultural Revolution, he was killed by the Red Guards—someone hit him over the head with a wooden board, and a nail pierced his skull.

—That's all in the past; it wouldn't happen now.

—The Red Guards gathered in Red Flag Square, then they split in two, and one group marched, singing, to our home, one to the other professor's. Those who came to ours left my father half-deaf and confiscated all his books. The other group beat the man to death, then scattered without ransacking his house.

—Yes, there was no telling how these things would turn out.

—I only found out about this later, after I was married and had Little Shu.

—Mm.

—The man who beat my father's friend to death was Zhuang Dezeng.

He was quiet for a moment, then he stood up. —You shouldn't be telling me this.

—I've finished now.

—The past has nothing to do with the present. People

change—we eat and drink and shit it out, the new replaces the old. And once a person has changed, you have to see the good in them. Zhuang isn't like that anymore.

—I know. I do know that. Won't you sit down again?

—No, I have to go fetch Fei. We should look to our own lives. Maybe you should think about being nicer to your son.

—Will you really not sit down? I feel uncomfortable, seeing you pace around like that.

—No, there's no time left. Fei and I will always be grateful to you, but we must follow our own path and look ahead—it's far too exhausting to keep looking back. You know the saying: If you had eyes in the back of your head, how would you ever move forward?

The days kept advancing, *tick-tick*, but I stayed behind. Everything moved on, *tick-tick*. I never saw Old Li or Fei again.

LI FEI

I sat by the window watching the sunlight dance on a poplar leaf. A day ago at this exact time, I was in this same spot, watching the light touch a different leaf. Autumn had arrived. The number of leaves was dwindling. I wanted to draw them but worried that I wouldn't capture their likeness, so I let them remain on the tree. This tree had been my companion for a long time. Every time I came here for treatment on my legs, I'd sit and look at it afterward, watching it slowly grow taller and thicker, its burgeoning crown waving in the wind, until the leaves fell and it was bare again.

I thought of the first time we moved. That wasn't our only

relocation, but it always hurts the most the first time. We lost most of our furniture, and the new place was half the size of the old one. The kang was cold when we moved in, and when my father lit the stove, there was a huge bang, flinging me into the air—the flames had ignited the accumulated methane. Sometimes, I'd come home from school to sit on that unfamiliar kang, and what I thought about more than anything was Little Shu's house, that courtyard I went to all the time. When they were moving away from our street, I said:

—Little Shu, Christmas is almost here.

—Nonsense, it's still three months away.

—By the time Christmas comes, we won't be neighbors anymore.

—So what?

I knew the Zhuangs celebrated Christmas. Every year on Christmas Eve, Teacher Fu would wrap presents for all of us. One year, she gave me a notebook, and on the front page she wrote, *No one can live forever, but we can be together forever*. I didn't understand the meaning, but I liked her handwriting, which was forceful and upright, like a man's. I asked Shu:

—What do you want?

—As if you could afford it. Besides, my mom would scold me if I took anything from you.

—I can make you something.

—Like what?

—How about fireworks?

—Like that time you set that matchbox alight?

—You still remember?

—That was nothing to brag about.

—You want something bigger?

He reached his hands as wide apart as they would go.
—The bigger the better.

I thought about it. —There's a sorghum field at the east
end of the city. In the winter, the stalks wither, and they'd light
up like a Christmas tree.

—Would you dare?

—Maybe we can set a whole patch on fire.

Shu clapped his hands. —Would you really dare?

—Come watch. Go past Coal-Fired Plant Number Four
and you'll see it.

—I'll dare if you'll dare.

—No matter where you are?

—No matter where I am.

—What if Teacher Fu doesn't let you come?

—Don't worry about that, I'll find a way.

—What time?

—Not too early or someone might see. Eleven o'clock?

—Eleven o'clock, don't forget.

—My memory is great, it's just whether or not I choose to
remember.

As I sat looking at the tree after my treatment, Tianbo
came over and started talking to me. Something about my
legs, I think, but I wasn't really following, still caught up in
those distant events. All those years ago, Teacher Fu sketching
a cigarette packet design while I knelt beside her, watching. It
was winter, and the kang was blazing hot. I was in a sweater
my father had knitted me, no socks. Teacher Fu stepped back
to look at me, smiled, and said: —Your dad's not a bad knitter.

I laughed, thinking of how clumsy my father looked with
the needles. I would sit next to him as he was winding the
wool and somehow got it tangled around his neck.

—Don't move, I'm drawing you.

—I'm going to be on a cigarette packet?

—I'm just trying something out, seeing if I can capture you and the sweater. Don't move.

When she was done with her sketch, I crawled over to look. It was me, sitting on the kang in my sweater, barefoot, throwing three shagai bones, which hung in midair like stars.

—What should we call this?

I looked at myself and couldn't think of anything.

—I know, it can be "The Plain."

Even though I didn't know what playing shagai had to do with plains, the name sounded good.

Another night many years ago, I woke up in one of the beds here. Tianbo approached. We'd met before, but not exchanged words. We weren't the talking sort. He stopped at my bed. Playing cards were laid out, long lines from king to ace, turning a corner when they reached the edge of the blanket. I was confused—I couldn't feel anything below my waist—and my back hurt badly.

—Tianbo, where's my dad?

—Oh, you're awake. He's fine, he's outside smoking with my dad. Are you playing cards?

—Where's my bag?

He pointed. It was on the other bed, with my bloody clothes.

—Help me get rid of it; I don't want my dad to see.

I realized Tianbo was repeating himself. Snapping out of my memories, I managed to take in his words:

—Your left leg seems thicker today.

—I guess it's swollen.

—No, it's gaining weight. During acupuncture just now, your nerves were more active. Try moving your toe.

I tried, but nothing happened. —You're wrong.

—Does your ankle feel warm?

—A little.

—That's a good sign. We'll keep an eye on it.

—You shouldn't cling to hope—it's unhealthy.

—I have a good reason—I started to see some changes last month. A spinal injury wouldn't normally heal, but you've been recovering. Your body has reflexes that weren't there before. It's strange, but everything works in its own way, and we'll just have to wait and see.

—It's nice and sunny out—take me for a walk.

—I have something to tell you: the police came by yester-day.

—Did you tell my dad?

—Yes, he said it's fine. By the way, I found a cigarette packet on the street yesterday; I'm guessing you don't have this one.

He reached into the right pocket of his white coat and fished out a flattened packet. I took it. Sure enough, it wasn't in my collection.

—Look at this little girl, how nicely she's drawn.

I tucked it between the pages of my book. —What did the police officers say?

—One of them was around forty, the other maybe twenty-two. They asked if I knew that a car accident had happened nearby twelve years ago, one where a policeman got shot. I told them I hadn't heard about that, but I was a kid then, so I was probably already in bed. They asked if my father had ever mentioned anything. I said no, he usually went to sleep early, too. I shared our medical records at their request, and when they were done looking, they asked to have a chat with my mother. I said after my father lost his job, my parents got divorced, and now I didn't know where she was or what she was doing. Then they left.

—Weren't you scared?

—I'm a doctor, after all . . . though maybe you shouldn't come here for a while, or call either. Let's wait for this to blow over. I'll give you a three-month supply of medicine, and remember to massage your legs the way I showed you.

—All right.

—Are you still writing your novel?

—Yes. I'm not done yet—I'll show you when I'm finished.

—Have a rest; I need to see another patient. The hot compress has been on half an hour, so you're almost done.

ZHUANG SHU

In the end, Commander Mo and I decided to go visit Jiang Bufan's mother. It might be a dry well, but why not stick our hands in to find out? We'd revisited the burning case and hadn't found anything suspicious. Just a single mother and daughter. They'd received a lot of donations from the public, and the girl's recovery was going better than expected—she was doing well at school. I doubted they'd have the motive or the ability to carry out a crime like the murder of two city officials. There was no link with the old cases, either. We did learn something from Sun Tianbo, which cheered Commander Mo. What we found was: nothing. Sun Tianbo's clinic was spotless, not a speck of dust anywhere. Medical records, silk pennants,

sandbags, acupuncture needles, medicinal herbs, beds, everything exactly in its place, plus two pots of African jasmine as
tall as a person. The medical records took up more than ten
volumes, with two people's handwriting, one more of a scrawl,
the other neat and workmanlike. As we headed back to our
vehicle, I said: —Dr. Sun's a little too perfect.

—What do you think we should do next?

—Track down Jiang Bufan's mother.

—Someone from the precinct can do that.

—Is any of his stuff still around?

—His mother kept his clothes, still bloody—she never
washed them. She said they're not dirty, just covered with her
son's blood.

Jiang Bufan's mother lived with her eldest daughter in Shashan District, to the west of the city, an undeveloped area—it
sat at the meeting point of three administrative regions, and
because all three wanted to manage it, none of them did. One
parcel of land had been slated for development, but after the
houses were leveled, nothing happened. Ten years later, it was
still just a hole in the ground, known locally as the Shashan
Pit. Mother and daughter operated a mahjong parlor next to
the Pit, just six tables and a kitchen so the gamblers could
order from the two-item menu: fried rice or fried noodles.
When we showed up, the daughter had gone to fetch her
child, and old Mrs. Jiang was watching the shop on her own,
snacking on sunflower seeds and chatting with one of the old
guys, who was saying:

—My pension's gone up a hundred and fifty yuan, not bad
at all—I'll have an extra pair of underpants to wear when I'm
dead.

Commander Mo said: —Not playing, ma'am?

She turned. —Ah, Xiaodong, you're here.

I handed over the bag of fruit I'd brought.

—I'm old, I don't eat this stuff. Buy me something else next time.

—This is Officer Zhuang Shu. Let's talk in the back room.

—Did you catch him?

The four people around the table looked up at us.

—No, I just want to talk; I haven't been here for a while. Hey, sir, just finish the game. No point holding out for a big win—that five bamboo tile is never going to show up.

The old guys burst out laughing, then continued playing.

Sure enough, Jiang Bufan's clothes were still there. Mrs. Jiang had rolled them into a neat bundle, like a steamed bun. She said: —I've been thinking, this body of mine is falling apart, so I was going to burn these on Bufan's death anniversary this year; otherwise they might get tossed out when I die.

—Well, let's have a look.

I picked up each article of clothing and examined it carefully, finding nothing. The bloodstains were black, and the pockets had been emptied long ago. But the second time I picked up the trousers, I realized there was a hole in the right pocket, and feeling down the leg, I found something in the cuff, caught in the lining. When I borrowed a pair of scissors to cut it open, I found a cigarette butt. I fished it out and saw two words on the filter: "The Plain."

—Ma'am, do you remember what brand of cigarettes your son smoked?

—Great Production. I used to buy him two packs a day— you can't get them anymore.

I turned to Commander Mo. —Is that right?

—Yes, I smoked Great Production too. Then they stopped making them, so I switched to Red Pagoda Mountain, then to the Good of the Masses.

I handed him the cigarette butt. —So who does this belong to?

On the way back to the station, we stopped at a tobacconist to buy a packet of Plains, and smoked one each. I studied the packet, on which there was a girl playing shagai bones. Though the picture was small and her features unclear, I thought she looked strangely familiar. Judging by the logo, the workmanship was excellent. Commander Mo said:

—These have improved. We had these back then too, but they used to be terrible, and later they disappeared.

—They were bad?

—Yes, and expensive, so not many people smoked them. The brand was launched not long before Jiang's murder. What a shame we didn't know there was something in his trousers all these years.

—It's not your fault; there was a hole in the pocket. Officer Jiang must have asked the killer for a smoke, noticed the unusual brand, and saved the butt.

Commander Mo called a meeting the next day, though he didn't mention the cigarette butt, because that would have meant admitting a past mistake—no harm waiting till the case was solved before owning up. Instead, he wanted to talk about two things: first, we would now keep a round-the-clock watch on the Sun clinic, and second, we should track down Sun Tianbo's mother as quickly as possible.

A week's surveillance of the clinic turned up nothing—no suspicious patients, and Sun Tianbo didn't look like he was about to flee—but his mother did surface. She was called

Liu Zhuomei, and ran a small Sichuan restaurant in Beijing's Chaoyang District, near the Fourth Ring Road, serving noodles, cow stomach skewers, and mala hot pot. The restaurant owner was a Sichuan guy who'd had a food cart in our city back in the day; the cart held a huge pot of spicy broth billowing clouds of steam with plastic sheeting around it. She would come for his spicy soup; then when Sun Yuxin lost his Job, they ran off together. Commander Mo and I caught the red-eye to Beijing, which was in chaos because of the upcoming Olympics. Even we, two detectives, got searched again and again. It was after ten by the time we got to the restaurant— hardly anyone was there, just a few waiters huddled around a pot of noodles, watching the small TV set on the corner shelf as they ate. It was footage of the construction of the half-built Bird's Nest, which looked like such a mess it might have been half torn down instead. We checked our photo and spotted Liu Zhuomei at a table doing her accounts, a cigarette in her hand, licking a finger every time she needed to turn a page. Her hair was going white—it had been dyed, but bands of silver stuck out from between the flax. When we told her why we'd come, she didn't panic, just told the serving staff they should go home early so we could have a proper chat.

—You're from my hometown. My accent is all twisted now, but we're still from the same place.

Her husband emerged from the kitchen, a short middle-aged man in sneakers with frayed laces. He brewed us a pot of tea, and she said: —Can he go home?

—Sure, we just want to clear a few things up with you.

The man walked out the door but didn't go far—he squatted by the side of the road with his back to us and started smoking.

—When did you leave Shenyang?

—October 8, 1994.

—Tell us what happened.

—My husband was a carpenter at the tractor factory, and he lost his job in the first round of redundancies. He wanted to start a clinic with his severance, but I thought that would cost too much, what with renting a place and all the equipment. Besides, he didn't have a medical license. It was one thing practicing on the side, but if he actually opened a clinic, it might get shut down. He refused to find a job, and I wouldn't give him the money—I held on to our savings book—so he hit me. We didn't get on. He was always hitting me, quite hard, too. I was already close to my Sichuan guy then, so I said to him, I have some money, will you take me away from here? He answered, Even if you didn't have money, I'd still leave with you. October 8 was a rest day, and my husband went out. I made lunch for Tianbo and watched him eat it, then I asked if one day I happened to leave his father, which of us would he rather stay with? He stopped eating long enough to say, With Dad. That afternoon, I got the savings book and left.

—So you weren't anywhere near Shenyang on December 24, 1995.

—1995? By that time we were working in Shenzhen.

Commander Mo shot me a look. —The clinic is doing well now. Your son's taken over—your husband is dead.

Her face remained expressionless. —I didn't have any contact with them after leaving. Tianbo's had a mind of his own since the day he was born.

I said: —Did you take all the family's savings?

—Yes, even his severance. I stuffed ten yuan into Tianbo's pocket before I left.

—Then where did Sun get the money to open a clinic? From his parents?

—They'd been dead a long time by then, and his brothers and sisters were worse off than him.

—So where did the money come from?

—How would I know?

—Help us out—can you think of anyone?

She pondered a while. —He did have an old friend. If anyone lent my husband money, it would be him. They'd known each other since they were kids, got sent down together, came back to the city, started working at the factory at the same time. He wasn't a bad person, very steady; I wonder what he's doing now.

—Can you remember what he was called?

—His surname was Li—now, what was his name? His wife was dead, and he was raising their daughter alone.

—Please try to remember.

—Sorry, all I've got is his surname. The girl was the bookish sort, knew all sorts of Tang and Song dynasty poems by heart. I used to see her around when she was a kid. Her name was Fei.

MO XIAODONG

Sun Tianbo kept his mouth firmly shut. I sent in some of our most experienced interrogators, and they couldn't crack him. Just wouldn't talk. Tried sleep deprivation, but he wore out our guards and kept clinging on. I said, If you don't know, say you don't know, and we'll write that in your file. But he wouldn't even say "I don't know," just rubbed his neck.

We found a replacement doctor to keep the clinic open. Searched the office and the living space inside and out, and found nothing. One of our guys said, I've never seen anyplace so tidy, it feels like no one lives here. I asked Zhuang what we should do next. He'd come back from Beijing in low spirits. Not being allowed to smoke on the plane drove him a bit crazy, and he'd gone through half a pack of Plains on his way to the station.

After poring through the records of every woman named Li Fei in this city, we found one who fit the bill. Her father, Li Shoulian, a bench worker at the tractor factory, had vanished after he was made redundant. Li Fei had an elementary school record, but nothing after that. Both files ended in 1995. As things stood, Li Shoulian was a major suspect in both the cab driver and cop murders and the 2007 attacks on city officials. Even if Li Fei wasn't an accomplice, she would be an important witness. People leave traces as long as they're alive. We had no way of knowing if Li Fei was still in this world, but her father definitely was—he'd updated his ID card not long ago.

Zhuang said: —A lot happened to the Lis that year: father lost his job, daughter graduated elementary school, and their family friend Sun Yuxin asked to borrow money so he could start a clinic. Li Shoulian loyally lent his friend the money, so Li Fei couldn't go to high school.

—I don't understand.

—Back then, even if you had the top exam marks in the whole city, if you wanted to enroll in high school, you had to pay nine thousand yuan up front. I'm thinking Li Fei got a place, but Li Shoulian's money was all tied up in the clinic, and that's why he started robbing taxi drivers.

—That makes sense.

—Do you remember the first case? The driver had a knife in his glove compartment—he was ex-military, and kept it there for safety on the night shift. That first time might have been a mistake. Maybe Li's plan was to take the money and run, but the driver fought back, and he ended up with blood on his hands. So then he was an armed robber.

—Sure, that's possible, but why does it matter what actually happened that first time?

—My theory is that it was the same situation when he attacked our officer. He hadn't planned to carry out a robbery—he was probably just going to Sun's clinic to pay a New Year's visit, or one of them actually was sick. But they hailed Jiang Bufan's taxi, and Jiang found Li suspicious. The two men got out of the vehicle halfway there, and you know what happened next.

—Maybe Li Fei played a part in the robberies, too.

—She could have, but it's not very likely.

—Why not?

—Human nature—her father wouldn't have gotten her involved.

The next day, I led a team of officers to search Sun Tianbo's home again. It really was immaculate—probably he'd always been prepared for the moment when we'd swoop in. I gave orders to pull up the wooden floorboards—nothing. I thought we might as well keep on going, so we ripped apart anything that could be a hiding place. Finally we found a medicinal pillow, the sort with a layer of pebbles inside that's supposed to help you sleep. Under the pebbles was a blood-stained elementary school Chinese textbook and seventy-odd pages of a photocopied text. I held these things up in front of Sun Tianbo, but just like before, he didn't say anything, just rubbed his temples. I looked through the manuscript, which seemed to be some sort of story about neighbors in the same row of houses, what happened between the kids, what happened between the grown-ups, playing with caterpillars, marbles, folded bits of cardboard. Probably from the author's own childhood. I handed these over to Zhuang, who couldn't come up with any conclusions, either. He asked for a few days off. He couldn't take it anymore, he said, his body was falling apart. I agreed—he was young, and this was his first time on this sort of case; of course he needed some rest. I suggested that first he go meet Sun Tianbo, who was, after all, our only lead at the moment, but he said no, he was really too exhausted. Maybe a few days off would give him time to get his thoughts in order.

On his third day off, something happened in the afternoon that none of us expected. At the start of the year, we'd gone after some fugitives, though mostly that was a waste of money and effort—the ones we caught, even the killers among them, were pathetic, old and decrepit, or else drunkards. One of them, a fifty-one-year-old, had robbed the China Construction Bank on Qishan Road in 1996, and fled after killing a security guard with a sawed-off shotgun. We caught him in Wuyang County, Henan. He confessed to the robbery and murder, and asked if he could see the wife he'd left behind all those years ago. I didn't think much about that—if I tried to satisfy all their desires, I'd never do anything else. Zhuang had gone to find the man's wife, who was also in her fifties, remarried and living a good life, now retired and looking after her grandchildren. She didn't want to see her ex. Zhuang managed to persuade her to pose for a picture, which he then gave the suspect, along with a report on how she was doing. He accepted the photo but didn't say much. And now, months later, he was suddenly claiming he had urgent information, so I went to see him. He wanted to see Zhuang. Zhuang's on leave, I said, he's not well—but I'm his superior officer, I can speak for him. The man recognized me and agreed to talk. I got him to write it down, then summoned the team so he could tell it all again.

His memory was excellent—the written account and both of his oral ones were completely consistent, and he remembered plenty of details from events that happened over ten years ago. His name was Zhao Qingge; he was unemployed, addicted to gambling and strong liquor. He could scan a tableful of mahjong tiles with a single glance and remember the position of each one after they were scrambled into walls. Even so, he still managed to lose, and ended up owing a lot of money. To crawl out of the hole he'd dug himself into, he started robbing taxi drivers. He was tall, five foot nine and very strong—by his own account, when he ate walnuts as a kid, he sometimes cracked them with his bare hands. Nylon rope, kerosene, sit right behind the driver, kill and rob him after getting to a remote spot, set the car on fire and run away. Five cases, and he remembered the time and place of each one, plus the appearance and age of every driver, and even what catchphrases some of them used. One of them had a comb in his pocket and kept smoothing his hair as he drove. He said he had a date with his thirty-two-year-old girlfriend right after this; her husband was always away on business. Zhao took his comb after strangling him and was still using it to this day.

But on December 24, 1995, he said, he wasn't in Jiang Bufan's car; he'd gone to Guangzhou to buy a gun. By that point, he'd held up five taxis without a single hitch and was ready for a harder target: banks. I showed him pictures of Li Shoulian and Li Fei, but he said he'd never seen those people in his life.

I had a look at the comb and gave Zhuang a call, but his phone was turned off. Actually, there was nothing urgent—although there was a missing link in our case, nothing about the work we needed to do had changed.

LI FEI

I couldn't sleep after what I'd read. I kept the newspaper by my pillow and got up several times in the night to look at it again. Two days ago my father had said, Tianbo's in trouble; the African jasmine isn't in his window anymore. I knew a lot of things were about to happen, but I hadn't expected to hear from Shu. The next morning, I showed my father the paper. He glanced at it.

—That's a coincidence.

I said nothing.

—I know what you're thinking.

—What am I thinking?

—You're thinking, maybe it will be all right.

I nodded.

—I'm pretty sure Tianbo won't have said anything. I know him, and even if he had, they wouldn't put out an ad for us.

I nodded again.

—But it's still a coincidence.

—Dad, is there something you're not telling me?

—I have to go on shift. Just let me think about this.

My father's a taxi driver these days.

When he got home that night, I was in my wheelchair, still looking at the paper.

WANTED: Searching for childhood playmate, my friend and sister Fei, whom I haven't seen in so many years. I'm leaving the country permanently in a week's time. Please get in touch with me as soon as possible. Can't believe we're grown up now. Here's my phone number.

And beneath the phone number, a photograph: a little boy standing between two stones, a girl with her leg pulled back, ready to kick a ball.

My father took off his mask and went into the kitchen with the groceries. As we ate dinner, he said:

—The sunbird in the square is getting torn down.

—Oh, what are they building instead?

—Would you believe it? They're bringing back the Chairman's statue, the same one they tore down all those years ago. It's still in good condition—they've kept it all this while. The soldiers at his feet got smashed when they took him down, though, so they'll have to recast those. I wonder if there'll be as many as before.

I waited.

—I've thought about it. You should meet him. I was planning to investigate, but that might cause more trouble. Why don't you just go?

I fell forward, dropping my bowl and scattering rice everywhere. My father scooped me up and put me back in my wheelchair.

—Come with me, Dad, but let me see him alone.

—Think of somewhere you can leave easily if it doesn't go well.

—I've thought about it—we should meet on the water.

—That's good, in separate boats alongside each other.

—He won't be able to tell my legs don't work.

My father produced a handgun from his belt. —Keep this in your bag, but don't use it unless you absolutely have to. If you do shoot, be ruthless.

I stared at the gun. My father pulled another one from the back of his trousers. —We'll have one each; yours has seven bullets. Now wait here and I'll go buy you a SIM card.

With the new SIM card in my phone, I texted Shu, asking him to meet me at noon the next day in the middle of the artificial lake at Beiling Park. After I pressed Send, my father put the SIM card on the stove, and we watched it melt.

—If he doesn't show up tomorrow at noon, then that will be that. And if he does come, then you'll talk, and that will be that anyway. We have to move on. Promise me.

—I promise. Dad, I owe you too much.

—Don't talk like that. The two of you need to see each other. And afterward, we'll go on like before.

ZHUANG SHU

A boat bobbed in the center of the lake. I rowed in its direction. It wasn't a holiday, so no other boats were out on the water. A cold autumn wind was furrowing the surface in tiny wrinkles, as if something were trembling at its very heart. As I got closer, I could see Li Fei. She was wearing a red coat, a black scarf, jeans, and brown shoes, and her hair was in a ponytail. A pair of gloves lay on top of the black shoulder bag at her feet. She looked very much like when she was twelve, with the same distinctive features, just a couple of sizes larger, and her hair was starting to go gray, blending with the willow catkins, though this didn't make her seem old. Her eyes never left me. I said:

—Have you been waiting long?

—No, it took me a while to row here.

—You haven't changed.

—You neither, except for the beard. Coming to see an old friend, and you couldn't be bothered to shave.

I laughed. —What are you up to these days?

—Asking questions right away? What about you?

—The truth?

—The truth.

—I'm a police officer.

Her lips pressed into a line. —That's good, public service.

—I was a little thug, wasn't I?

She was silent for a while. —You were.

—Now that I'm grown up, I want to protect other people.

She didn't say anything for a long time, just rearranged the scarf around her neck. Finally, she spoke. —Is Teacher Fu doing well?

—Very well—she's been all over the globe.

—Is that good?

—To be honest, I don't know. She never stopped searching for you.

—Tell her to stop searching, I'm nothing at all.

—I disagree. If you're not in a hurry, I'll tell you what I've been doing all these years.

—Go ahead.

So I told her everything, all the girlfriends I'd had at the academy, how sad I felt each time we broke up, getting drunk and running around the track like a madman, how I'd become much closer to my dad after qualifying as an officer. She paid close attention, asking a detailed question now and then—it's rare to find such a good listener. When I was done, I felt like I'd had a shower.

—How pointless, all these years, and it hardly took me any time to tell you what I've done.

—If I did the same, it would just be one sentence.

—Are you going back on your own after this? Or is Uncle Li nearby, watching us?

Silence.

—What's he up to these days?

Silence.

—Twelve years ago, Uncle Li killed five taxi drivers. More recently, he murdered two city officials, one with a hammer or wrench, one with a gun.

Silence.

—I'm not asking for your help; I'm asking you to think about these actual crimes.

—Is this really necessary?

—Tell me where I can find Uncle Li; then you can get into my boat and we'll row back to shore together. We can go see your Teacher Fu.

—If these things hadn't happened, would you still have tried to find me?

—Perhaps not. But I've come alone today, and no one knows I'm here. Besides, these things did happen, and I did find you.

She grabbed her oars and sent her boat backward, a little away from me. She said:

—Actually, I could have said I don't know what you're talking about, but you were very honest with me, so I'll be honest with you, too—that way we won't owe each other anything. Or no, that's wrong: I should have said I owe your family so much, so this is a way of paying back a little.

—No, this is between you and me—

She lifted her hand for silence. After all these years, something about her had changed.

—Those cab murders in 1995 had nothing to do with my father, whether you believe it or not. He lent some of his savings to Uncle Sun, and then he sold all the Cultural Revolution stamps he'd collected as a child, which brought in enough for my school fees. But on December 24, I was with him. That man shot my father, and the bullet went through his left cheek.

—Oh.

—A truck hit the car I was in and flipped it over. Did you know that?

—Yes, I did.

—Then the other man was on the ground, and my dad came over with his face covered in blood to drag me out. My mind was very clear. When my dad saw my legs, he left me at the side of the road, and went back to smash the other man's head in with a brick.

—So that's what happened.

—Just before I fainted, I told him, Shu is waiting for me.

Now I was the silent one. I looked into her unblinking eyes.

—My dad doesn't know anything; he thinks I really did

have a stomachache that night. I had a bottle of kerosene in my schoolbag—he'd brought it back from the factory to clean our windows. I guess the policeman smelled it. It was Christmas Eve. All day long, I'd wondered whether I should go, because I had a feeling you wouldn't show up. But evening came, and I decided to do it, only I couldn't think how. You said you always find a way. Then I thought of Uncle Sun's clinic near the sorghum field—I could somehow slip out of the taxi and set it alight with the kerosene, a whole field of Christmas trees, just like I promised you.

—The sorghum field isn't there anymore.

—Did you go, that day?

—No.

—Teacher Fu wouldn't let you?

—No, I forgot.

—What did you do instead?

—I can't remember.

She nodded and pointed at her shoulder bag. —I have a gun in here, but I have no idea if I can use it.

—If you can't, I'll teach you.

—When I was a girl, Teacher Fu told me a story, about how as long as your faith is strong enough, the ocean will part and make a path for you to cross. There's no ocean here, but if you can make the lake waters part, I'll let you board my boat, and I'll leave with you.

—No one can do that.

—I want the lake to part.

I thought about it. —I can't part the waters, but I can turn them into a plain.

—That's impossible.

—And if I can?

—I'll come with you.

—Are you ready?

—I'm ready.

I reached into my jacket, past my handgun, and got the packet of cigarettes. That was our plain. There she was, eleven or twelve years old, barefoot and smiling, staring into space. The packet floated on the lake, its plastic wrapper glinting in the sunlight, the northern afternoon breeze tugging at her, wafting her gently back to shore.

SHUANG XUETAO is one of the most highly celebrated young Chinese writers. Born in 1983 in the city of Shenyang, Shuang has written six volumes of fiction, for which he has won the Blossoms Literary Prize, the Wang Zengqi Short Story Prize, and the Blancpain-Imaginist Literary Prize for the best Chinese writer under forty-five. His short stories and novellas, including "Moses on the Plain," have been adapted into major television productions and feature films. Shuang lives in Beijing.

JEREMY TIANG has translated over twenty works from the Chinese by authors such as Zhang Yueran, Yan Ge, and Geling Yan. For these translations he has received a PEN/Heim Grant, an NEA Literature Translation Fellowship, and a Mao-Tai Cup for Translation. His novel, *State of Emergency*, won the Singapore Literature Prize in 2018. He also writes and translates plays. Originally from Singapore, Tiang lives in Flushing, Queens.

MADELEINE THIEN is the acclaimed author of four books of fiction, which have been translated into more than twenty-five languages. *Do Not Say We Have Nothing*, her most recent novel, received Canada's two highest literary honors, the Giller Prize and the Governor-General's Literary Award for Fiction, and was short-listed for the Booker Prize, the Women's Prize for Fiction, and the Folio Prize.

SHUANG XUETAO is one of the most highly celebrated young Chinese writers. Born in 1983 in the city of Shenyang, Shuang has written six volumes of fiction, for which he has won the Blossoms Literary Prize, the Wang Zengqi Short Story Prize, and the Blancpain-Imaginist Literary Prize for the best Chinese writer under forty-five. His short stories and novellas, including "Moses on the Plain," have been adapted into major television productions and feature films. Shuang lives in Beijing.

JEREMY TIANG has translated over twenty works from the Chinese by authors such as Zhang Yueran, Yan Ge, and Geling Yan. For these translations he has received a PEN/Heim Grant, an NEA Literature Translation Fellowship, and a Mao-Tai Cup for Translation. His novel, *State of Emergency*, won the Singapore Literature Prize in 2018. He also writes and translates plays. Originally from Singapore, Tiang lives in Flushing, Queens.

MADELEINE THIEN is the acclaimed author of four books of fiction, which have been translated into more than twenty-five languages. *Do Not Say We Have Nothing*, her most recent novel, received Canada's two highest literary honors, the Giller Prize and the Governor-General's Literary Award for Fiction, and was short-listed for the Booker Prize, the Women's Prize for Fiction, and the Folio Prize.